Clint Adams never drew his gun unless it was absolutely necessary, but he was out of options. His punches against the big man did as much damage as a tuft of straw swatting against a side of beef.

The Colt filled Clint's hand after a quick flicker of motion from his right arm. Its weight gave Clint a healthy dose of confidence that he would walk away from the scuffle without getting his limbs torn from their sockets.

That confidence lasted right up until the big man reached out and swatted away the gun as though he was relieving a child of his toy.

"That ain't fair," the big man said. "Now you gone and made me angry . . ."

DON'T MISS THESE
ALL-ACTION WESTERN SERIES
FROM THE BERKLEY PUBLISHING GROUP

THE GUNSMITH by J. R. Roberts

Clint Adams was a legend among lawmen, outlaws, and ladies. They called him . . . the Gunsmith.

LONGARM by Tabor Evans

The popular long-running series about Deputy U.S. Marshal Long—his life, his loves, his fight for justice.

SLOCUM by Jake Logan

Today's longest-running action Western. John Slocum rides a deadly trail of hot blood and cold steel.

BUSHWHACKERS by B. J. Lanagan

An action-packed series by the creators of Longarm! The rousing adventures of the most brutal gang of cutthroats ever assembled—Quantrill's Raiders.

DIAMONDBACK by Guy Brewer

Dex Yancey is Diamondback, a Southern gentleman turned con man when his brother cheats him out of the family fortune. Ladies love him. Gamblers hate him. But nobody pulls one over on Dex . . .

WILDGUN by Jack Hanson

The blazing adventures of mountain man Will Barlow—from the creators of Longarm!

TEXAS TRACKER by Tom Calhoun

Meet J.T. Law: the most relentless—and dangerous—manhunter in all Texas. Where sheriffs and posses fail, he's the best man to bring in the most vicious outlaws—for a price.

THE GUNSMITH

299

SNAKEBITE CREEK

J. R. ROBERTS

JOVE BOOKS, NEW YORK

THE BERKLEY PUBLISHING GROUP
Published by the Penguin Group
Penguin Group (USA) Inc.
375 Hudson Street, New York, New York 10014, USA
Penguin Group (Canada), 90 Eglinton Avenue East, Suite 700, Toronto, Ontario M4P 2Y3, Canada
(a division of Pearson Penguin Canada Inc.)
Penguin Books Ltd., 80 Strand, London WC2R 0RL, England
Penguin Group Ireland, 25 St. Stephen's Green, Dublin 2, Ireland (a division of Penguin Books Ltd.)
Penguin Group (Australia), 250 Camberwell Road, Camberwell, Victoria 3124, Australia
(a division of Pearson Australia Group Pty. Ltd.)
Penguin Books India Pvt. Ltd., 11 Community Centre, Panchsheel Park, New Delhi—110 017, India
Penguin Group (NZ), Cnr. Airborne and Rosedale Roads, Albany, Auckland 1310, New Zealand
(a division of Pearson New Zealand Ltd.)
Penguin Books (South Africa) (Pty.) Ltd., 24 Sturdee Avenue, Rosebank, Johannesburg 2196,
South Africa

Penguin Books Ltd., Registered Offices: 80 Strand, London WC2R 0RL, England

This is a work of fiction. Names, characters, places, and incidents either are the product of the author's imagination or are used fictitiously, and any resemblance to actual persons, living or dead, business establishments, events, or locales is entirely coincidental.

SNAKEBITE CREEK

A Jove Book / published by arrangement with the author

PRINTING HISTORY
Jove edition / November 2006

ISBN: 0-515-14219-0

JOVE®
Jove Books are published by The Berkley Publishing Group,
a division of Penguin Group (USA) Inc.,
375 Hudson Street, New York, New York 10014.
JOVE is a registered trademark of Penguin Group (USA) Inc.
The "J" design is a trademark belonging to Penguin Group (USA) Inc.

PRINTED IN THE UNITED STATES OF AMERICA

10 9 8 7 6 5 4 3 2 1

ONE

"String him up!"

That phrase sliced through the air like an arrow on an otherwise peaceful day. At first, it seemed as if it had come from nowhere and would disappear to that same place. Then, another voice was raised.

"Yeah," it shouted. "String him from that pole!"

Now, instead of just a voice being raised, a finger was lifted as well so it could point toward a telegraph pole that was splintered and crooked, but more than sturdy enough to do the job.

Standing in the middle of a growing mob, a slender man with neatly trimmed hair and a narrow face held up his hands and patted the air as if that would be enough to calm everyone down. "Now hold on a minute here," he said. "No need to get overly excited."

"Son of a bitch cheated me out of my savings!" yet another voice said. "I say we should break his legs first and then string him up!"

The man in the middle pulled in a breath as his eyes went wide. "That is completely uncalled for!"

"All right then," the first one to start screaming said. "We can just string you up and be done with it."

1

"There's law here," the man in the middle said. "In fact, I'd wager the law will be by here any moment, which means you should all disperse before you are brought up on charges. Lynching isn't exactly legal, you know."

"Lynching?" called a stout man with dark, greasy hair who shoved his way through the crowd. "Is that what you call it, Whiteoak? From where I'm standing it seems more like justice and that's what the law is all about the last time I checked."

Henry Whiteoak kept shifting on his feet and shuffling from one spot to another in an effort to get out from the middle of that mob. But the more he tried to wriggle away from those people, the more the mob shifted so they could stay around him.

Finally, Whiteoak planted his feet and straightened up as if he was just another one of the enraged bystanders. He wore a rumpled suit and had the sleeves of his starched white shirt rolled up to his bony elbows. A black string tie was wrapped around his neck at an odd angle. With all the talk of a hanging, he'd started nervously tugging at the tie as if it was the noose in question.

"Justice involves a trial and a judge," Whiteoak said. "Maybe then these folks would see that I deserve anything but a noose."

The man who'd called Whiteoak by name kept his spot at the inner ring of the crowd. He wore a suit as well, but had managed to keep his in somewhat better condition. It was made from silk, covered in pinstripes, and hung on his body without doing a bit of good to cover the bulky angles of the man's torso.

His eyes were like bits of coal that had been jammed into his sockets. Furrowed brows hung down low and were currently twisted into a smug, disbelieving scowl. "You expect anyone with half a brain to believe a damn word you say?"

"Of course I do," Whiteoak said with a firm nod. "Because it's the truth."

There was a moment of silence after that, which seemed to give Whiteoak a little hope. He kept his chin up and his hands firmly clasped onto his shirtfront as if he had lapels. His legs had even stopped shifting in his futile attempt to get away from all those focused stares.

After another moment slipped by, laughter started rippling through the crowd until it became something of a roar. In stark contrast, Whiteoak's face took on a deep, sorrowful tone.

"I guess these good people have cast their vote," the man with the cold eyes said. "You still want to wait for a trial by jury?"

Lowering his head, Whiteoak moved in a straight line directly toward the stout man who'd taken it upon himself to speak for the rest of the mob. He didn't get within five paces of the man before he was stopped by no less than four pistols aimed in his direction.

Once he saw Whiteoak begin to back away, the man with the cold eyes motioned for them to lower their guns. "Relax, boys. It seems our friend Mr. Whiteoak wants to talk. Maybe he wants to discuss the law some more?"

That got a good laugh from the crowd, and allowed the slender man in the rumpled suit to move a little closer to the man with cold eyes.

"This is all a misunderstanding, Cal," Whiteoak said. "And it's not just between me and these people."

"Oh, I'm certain it's a misunderstanding. These folks thought they were buying something other than piss oil when they gave you their money."

"It's not just that."

"There's also the land sales," Cal continued. "And some gambling debts you racked up in my place. My gut tells me there's plenty more that I don't even know about."

"That's not what all this fuss is about, though."

Cal Teasley fixed a stern glare on Whiteoak and held it there until the other man started to squirm.

"All right," Whiteoak groaned. "Maybe its what some of it is about, but not all."

"Some is enough to get a man hanged. Hell, oftentimes it takes less than that to stretch a neck."

Glancing nervously between Teasley and the rest of the crowd, Whiteoak leaned forward even though he could feel the hackles raising on those four gunmen's necks. "This thing is bound to get worse before it gets better. For you and me."

Teasley leaned in as if to mock Whiteoak's previous movements. "I'd say things look a whole lot worse for you than they do for me," he said in a stage whisper that could be easily heard by anyone in the vicinity. Dropping his voice to a genuine whisper, he added, "And cutting into my gambling business didn't help you none either."

Whiteoak's eyes grew even wider as every last bit of color drained from his face. Hearing those words were similar to having a cold rake dragged across his bare spine. "I . . . I didn't—"

"Don't bullshit me," Teasley snarled under his breath. "You stepped on the wrong set of toes when you started swindling my customers."

"But it won't be long before—"

Teasley snapped his fingers, which caused two of his gunmen to grab hold of Whiteoak's arms and haul him off his feet. "Ain't nobody comes into my place and starts acting like they own it. Far as I'm concerned, you lost every bit of sympathy from me once you pulled that shit."

Rather than fight against the men that were holding him, Whiteoak felt himself start to relax and dangle from their grip like a fish that had been dangling from a hook for too long. He wasn't buying into what Teasley was saying, simply because that one's eyes were incapable of ever showing the first hint of sympathy. Whiteoak had at least figured he could bargain with the man.

Until now.

Only one thing seemed certain anymore inside White-oak's mind. It was so certain, in fact, that he didn't even need to hear the words spoken out loud.

Playing up to the crowd, Teasley spoke them anyway. "String him up."

TWO

Henry Whiteoak carried an old revolver on him most of the time, but that had been stripped from his waist the moment the mob got its hands on him. Even though he'd felt his weapon being taken, Whiteoak had known better than to resist. Doing so would have only given the mob an excuse to start punching and kicking on top of everything else they were already doing.

As Whiteoak was dragged down the street, Teasley watched with an amused grin on his face.

"What the hell's going on here?" a younger man asked as he pushed his way through the unruly mob.

Teasley shifted until he got a look at who was trying to interrupt, and then relaxed when he saw who it was. "Take it easy, Deputy. We're just conducting a bit of business here."

The deputy was a good-sized man with bulky arms and two guns around his waist. Since Teasley's men were so close, however, he knew better than to draw either of those guns. "I hear there's a man that's to be hung."

"You heard right."

"Last time I checked, that was a duty to be carried out by the sheriff."

"We're saving the sheriff some trouble as well as a few dollars that could be better spent in fixing the boardwalks around town," Teasley said as he struck something of a mayoral pose.

"The sheriff won't like the sound of that."

Although it wasn't much for Teasley to shift from his normal expression to a threatening snarl, the difference in his voice was striking. "Then he don't have to know about it," he said in a deep rasp that reminded the deputy of a wolf guarding a fresh kill.

Hearing that was more than enough to bring Teasley's men in around the deputy like the rope that was being cinched around Whiteoak's neck. Even though they put their hands on their pistols and stalked forward earnestly, the gunmen weren't able to back the deputy down completely.

"The sheriff will hear about this one way or the other," the lawman said. "He's the one that sent me down to see what all this commotion was about."

"Then report back to him that we're just having a friendly little debate about the application of justice."

Having spotted the badge among the sea of angry faces, Whiteoak squirmed and wriggled until he was able to lock eyes with the deputy. "Whatever I did, I'll answer for it!"

"What did he do?" the deputy asked.

Teasley took his time in choosing his words as the rest of the mob found something that was strong enough to support Whiteoak's weight and tall enough to get the job done. "I'm not the formal leader of these proceedings, but I know there's several charges being tossed about."

As the deputy tried to get a better look at what was going on, he asked, "What charges?"

"Theft and cheating, for one. Maybe swindling is in there as well."

"Isn't that the salesman that rode into town a week ago?"

"One and the same."

"Then anyone with any sense knows better than to trust everything he says."

Teasley shrugged while positioning himself to stand between the deputy and a clear look at the mob's activities.

"You folks there!" the deputy shouted. "Step away from that man and take a moment to think, for Christ's sake!"

Just as it seemed that a good amount of the crowd was beginning to heed the lawman's advice, a few of Teasley's gunmen stepped up to knock the deputy back.

"I suggest you do the walking and let the wheels of justice go through their proper motions," Teasley said.

There was a fire in the deputy's eyes that made it clear he wanted to finish what he'd started. The muscles under his skin were taut and his fists were clenched as if he'd already committed himself to a fight. But his brain was keeping him from throwing himself into that fight simply because he knew he probably wouldn't make it out.

Teasley's men were itching for that same fight and they outnumbered the deputy four to one. That was assuming there weren't more gunmen nearby who would jump at the chance to come to their partners' side if push came to shove.

Starting a fight was easy enough, the deputy knew. Finishing it in one piece was a whole other thing entirely.

"Have it your way," the deputy said as he shook free of the gunmen. Turning on his heels, he left the crowd and headed down the street.

"You think he'll get the sheriff?" one of the gunmen asked.

Teasley nodded. "Either that, or he's off to round up some of those other deputies. Whichever it is, he'll be back. This shouldn't take too much longer, though. Just to be certain, why don't two of you make certain that boy finds his way back to where he needs to go?"

"And if he gets cross with us?" the gunman asked.

"Mind your manners. I don't pay the sheriff enough to

use his boys as target practice. If they do wind up getting some bumps and bruises, however . . ."

As two of the gunmen nodded and took off after the deputy, Teasley stepped forward to shove his way once more through the crowd. When he emerged out the other side, he saw Henry Whiteoak balanced precariously on top of a wobbly stack of crates with both hands tied behind his back.

"There's no need for this," Whiteoak said as one of the locals tossed a rope over the cross-arm of a telegraph pole. "I can just pack up and leave, if it's so important."

Teasley simply watched quietly as the noose was fitted around Whiteoak's neck.

THREE

When he saw Teasley's eyes snap up to the top of the pole, Whiteoak shook his wrists until the straight-edge he kept up his sleeve slipped into his waiting hand. As he eased the blade open and rubbed the edge against the ropes, Whiteoak wondered what the hell he could do even if he managed to break free.

Rather than try to figure out the odds stacked against him, Whiteoak got busy cutting.

Just as the blade became wedged deep within the rope around his left wrist, Whiteoak heard a voice coming from directly behind him.

"Hey! What's that in yer hand?"

Ignoring those words and the heavy footsteps that followed them, Whiteoak put even more force behind his efforts until his hand snapped free.

"Son of a bitch's got a knife!"

Every face in that crowd was already turned in Whiteoak's direction. Now, as if the move was perfectly timed, they all shifted from amusement to panic in the blink of an eye.

Whiteoak could feel his balance being threatened as the crates shifted under his feet. He didn't have time to worry about that, however, since he was more concerned with stretching his arm up to grab hold of the rope connecting his neck to that pole.

Just as his hand closed around the section of rope above his head, Whiteoak saw Teasley storm toward the crates like an angry bull. His face was beet red and his teeth were clenched as he snarled at his men.

"What the hell is wrong with you assholes?" Teasley growled. "Can't you even string up one skinny little prick without messing it up?"

Letting their actions speak for them, the two remaining gunmen drew their pistols so they could take aim and finish Whiteoak off the easy way.

Even though he saw those guns out of the corner of his eye, Whiteoak maintained his own focus and perched on his tiptoes on those crates. With one slash of his straight-edge, he cut through the rope and felt the glorious rush of air flowing into his lungs. Before he could take a full breath, Whiteoak felt his bottom half lurching out from underneath the rest of him.

Whiteoak landed with the small of his back against the edge of the top crate and then rolled off. While it had seemed like he was a mile up a few seconds ago, he found out soon enough that he'd only been five or six feet off the ground. His arm and ribs slammed against the ground, forcing the bit of air he'd sucked into his lungs to come rushing out in a single gasp.

At that moment, a shot blasted through the air to knock a hole through the crate that was second to the top of the stack. Wood splinters popped out the back of the crate and then fluttered down onto Whiteoak's shoulder, giving him even more of a reason to get his feet beneath him and force himself to move.

Just as Whiteoak thought he was going to stand up, his heel slid against the dirt and he fell backward once more. His first reflex was to catch himself with one arm before he took another hard spill onto his sore body. Fortunately, the hand he used to stop his fall wasn't the one wrapped around his straight-edge.

"Nice try, shithead," the gunman said as he pushed over the rest of the crates and swung his pistol around to point at Whiteoak. "But that's about as far as you're gonna go."

Instead of trying to get up again, Whiteoak dropped onto his side so he could extend his other arm to its limit. He snapped that arm forward like a whip, slicing through the air with the straight-edge.

For a sickening moment, Whiteoak knew his reach hadn't been long enough to do any damage.

Then, his opinion changed as he saw the gunman in front of him sway backward like a tree getting ready to fall over. And just like that same tree, the gunman wasn't able to keep from falling once he was headed in that direction.

The gunman fell straight back and landed with a solid thump. Once his back had hit the dirt, he didn't even make an attempt to get back up again. Instead, he reached out with his free hand to feel the spot just below his knee where there was a dark, wet patch of blood seeping through his pants.

Whiteoak looked down at the blade in his hand as though he still wasn't sure if he'd been the one to do that damage. Sure enough, the end of the straight-edge was glistening with blood. The blade was so sharp that he hadn't even felt it cut through the meat of the gunman's leg.

"You're . . . dead!" the gunman shouted as he lifted his pistol in an unsteady hand. The first shot he took dug into the dirt a good four feet from where Whiteoak was lying. After a few fumbling attempts to pull the trigger again, the gunman took another shot that was a little closer to the mark.

Before he knew what he was doing, Whiteoak was on his feet and stumbling away from the now panicked mob. More shots were blasting through the air, but they would have had to take Whiteoak's head clean off his shoulders in order to slow him down.

Behind Whiteoak, Teasley sighted along the barrel of his gun before thinking twice about pulling his trigger again. When he saw that the other two gunmen weren't thinking so clearly, he reached out and roughly smacked both men's hands down.

"You want us to be taken in for murder?" Teasley asked angrily.

The gunmen blinked in confusion before one of them asked, "Weren't we gonna hang him?"

"Not him, idiot! Them!"

Now, both gunmen looked at the locals that were stampeding like spooked cattle. Most of those folks were well within their line of fire. Seeing that, the gunmen lowered their pistols.

"Should we go after him?"

"Nah," Teasley replied. "I didn't see where he slithered off to. Did either of you?"

Rather than give an answer Teasley didn't want, both gunmen simply kept their mouths shut.

"All right then," Teasley said. "That little prick's too scared to come back anyway. Let's head back to the Dollar so these assholes can buy each other some drinks. Speaking of assholes . . ."

As Teasley's words trailed off, he and his men turned their backs to the group of lawmen who were rushing straight toward them.

FOUR

The deputy had returned, but now he had a few partners as well as an older man whose badge looked slightly more official than the dented tin pinned to the younger men's chests.

Even though he was older than his deputies, the sheriff wasn't an old man. He was in his mid-thirties, but carried his age gracefully and looked more like someone in his twenties. There was an intensity in his eyes, however, that had only gotten there after seeing too much of the world's harsh ways.

"What the hell's going on here?" the sheriff asked. "What's all the shooting about?" Since there were no answers forthcoming, the sheriff gave some quick orders to his deputies, who then rounded up some members of the crowd. The sheriff walked right up to Teasley and grabbed hold of the man's shoulder.

"I asked you a question, Teasley."

Teasley sucked in a breath and turned around to show the lawman a crooked smile. "I came along when this was well in progress, Sheriff Morton. I'm sure your deputy can attest to that."

"If I wanted to hear from one of my deputies, I'd be

14

talking to them. I heard there was a lynching going on here."

"There was, but it was well justified."

Sheriff Morton nodded warily as he glanced around at the locals who were scattering like so many frightened deer. "Does this have to do with that snake-oil salesman who just tore out of town with his horse and wagon?"

"You let him go?" Teasley fumed.

"Didn't have any reason not to," Sheriff Morton replied with a grin of his own. "Maybe you'll inform me of your intentions next time you take part in distributing your own justice around here."

With a great deal of effort, Teasley backed down and forced a somewhat casual air into his manner. "Of course, Sheriff. Anything you say." He then turned away from the lawmen.

Although he'd been trying to contain himself so far, Teasley's facade cracked like a layer of cheap paint as he turned back and snarled, "The bastard came into my place and started fleecing my customers. Not to mention all the cons he's been pulling that have had him selling everything from miracle cures to raw opium."

Sheriff Morton's expression shifted as well, but it was more in the way of gaining control instead of losing it. "Considering how much opium you sell from under that bar of yours, I'll bet that really got under your skin."

"That's a dirty trade and an even dirtier accusation," Teasley shot back. "Especially since you can't prove a damn thing."

"Not yet anyway."

"Well, I'm not the one that deserves to be strung up. Just ask these people. At least, you could if they weren't scared off when that maniac tried to gut my associate. Just take a look at his leg!"

Sheriff Morton glanced over at the gunman who was being helped up by one of his partners. Every time the man put a bit of weight on his leg, he grunted with pain. Even so, he still managed to make his way on his own after a few failed attempts.

"Looks like it could have been a lot worse," Morton said. "Especially since I heard more than a few gunshots coming from over here."

"He went crazy rather than accept his punishment."

"That's not your call to make. A judge will decide if any punishment is in order."

"Wasn't my call, Sheriff. As you can see, there were plenty of folks here to get this party going."

Without taking his eyes from Teasley's intense stare, Sheriff Morton said, "If you're not careful, you might just get a party like this of your own."

"Take your best shot," Teasley snapped. "And good luck finding a judge or any other official in this state to back your play. Now if you'll excuse me, I have to make sure that escaped lunatic hasn't already burned down my saloon just for the hell of it." With that, Teasley put his back to the sheriff again and stormed away.

"You just going to let him turn his back to you like that?" one of Morton's deputies asked.

The sheriff winced and replied, "He's all bluster so long as he doesn't have a mob behind him. I'd say we put enough fear into whoever was present that they won't want to follow his lead anytime soon."

"Everyone but those gunhands on his payroll maybe."

"He'll do what he does and we'll do what we do. That's about all the certainty we got. Just to be safe, why don't you and Seth check in at the Silver Dollar to see what's got Teasley's feathers so ruffled. That salesman must have done something a whole lot worse than steal from a devil like Teasley to call down this big of a shit storm."

FIVE

The Sacramento River snaked into the horizon just outside
Clint's window. It was just quiet enough at the outskirts of
town for him to hear the water trickling over the rocks if he
just took a moment to listen for it. Over the last few days,
he'd been taking plenty of moments to do just that.

Although he tried to look for places just like the
Riverview Hotel whenever possible, he rarely got the opportunity to enjoy them to their fullest. Usually, Clint was
nursing a wound or two while settling in after being chased
or shot at by someone or other. Unfortunately, this time
was no different.

The wounds he was recovering from weren't exactly
life-threatening, but they did add to the continual flow of
aches or pains that nagged at him for any variety of reasons.

When it was about to rain, an old bullet wound let him
know.

A scar from a particularly bad knife fight acted up when
the air got too cold.

Bruised ribs groaned if he slept badly.

The list went on and on, but that was all to be expected
for living the life he'd chosen for himself. At moments like
this, on the other hand, every one of those aches and pains

17

seemed worth it to be able to take some time for himself without having to plan or save up years in advance.

A knock on his door jarred Clint from his thoughts, while also reminding him of another problem with taking time to catch his breath.

Without fail, someone always seemed to track him down.

"Who is it?" Clint asked without taking his eyes from the little bit of whitewater he'd spotted from his window.

The voice that drifted through the door was every bit as smooth and inviting as warm silk sheets. "It's Sadie."

As much as Clint wanted to enjoy his peace and quiet, Sadie Lensher had been a very welcome distraction. The subtle German accent in the woman's voice had a way of drifting over Clint's skin like the painted nails at the ends of her fingers.

"Come on in," he said.

The door opened and Sadie walked inside. She wore a light-colored blouse that wasn't quite thick enough to keep him from noticing the darker-colored corset beneath it. As always, her golden hair looked perfectly tended while also being freshly tussled. Thick, soft lips curled into an apologetic smile as her blue eyes quickly looked Clint up and down.

"Hope I didn't interrupt," she said.

Clint smirked and replied, "Does it look like I'm doing anything important?"

"No, but I know you didn't want everyone knowing you were here."

Being known as The Gunsmith throughout a good part of the country could have its advantages. It also had more than its share of disadvantages, which was why Clint didn't go around advertising who he was so every drunken would-be gunfighter could hunt him down. He didn't lie about it, but he preferred to keep quiet about it just in case anyone was looking to make a name for themselves.

"Is someone asking for me?" Clint asked.

Sadie shook her head and fished a folded envelope from the pocket of her light blue skirt. "This arrived for you," she said while handing it over.

"Usually the mail is kept at the front desk. It must be important."

"This didn't come by mail. It was delivered by hand a few minutes ago to the front desk. The man who brought it said to deliver it straight to you if you were staying here."

Clint studied Sadie's face and then shifted his eyes to the letter that was still in her hand. "He delivered it here, so he must know I'm here."

"I don't think he's sure about it, since he delivered a letter to the Pearl right before coming here."

The Pearl and the Riverview were the only two hotels in town, which loosened the knot in Clint's stomach a little.

"So he probably suspects I'm in town, but doesn't know for sure," Clint said, thinking out loud.

Sadie nodded. "He looked hopeful. He even said he was a friend of yours."

Although he wasn't about to let down his guard all the way, Clint took a small bit of comfort from hearing that. Then again, the devil himself got a long way by claiming to be someone's friend. "Let's see that letter," he said.

Sadie handed it over and Clint took it from its envelope. He only needed to read a few lines of it before rolling his eyes and groaning under his breath. "I don't believe this."

"What's the matter? Is it bad? Should I have just thrown it away?"

"No, it's not bad. It's not exactly good, but you did the right thing."

"Do you know this man?"

"Yeah. Unfortunately."

"He seemed harmless," Sadie explained. "He even seemed a little frightened. I . . . I felt sorry for him, so I took the letter, but I didn't tell him I knew where you were. I waited until he left before I brought the letter to you."

Without reading the rest of the letter, Clint reached out and put a hand on her shoulder. "Don't worry about it, Sadie. You didn't do anything wrong. I wouldn't have gotten to know the man who wrote this letter unless I'd felt sorry for him the first time we crossed paths."

"Did he try to hurt you?"

"Not directly, no. But enough trouble brews around him that it might have been better if he did just try to take a shot at me and be done with it."

Although she'd been starting to brighten up, Sadie lowered her eyes again when she heard that. "I'll put the letter back where it was and say I never saw you. I promise you won't be bothered."

Clint placed a finger under her chin and lifted her face so he could look deeply into her blue eyes. "You're sweet and there was no harm done. Whatever you heard about men coming after me is mostly a bunch of rumors started in saloons."

Although that was a bit of a fib on Clint's part, it was enough to bring the smile back to Sadie's face and that was more than enough to make it worthwhile.

"Did the man who brought that letter say anything else?" Clint asked.

After a bit of thinking, Sadie replied, "Just that he was renting a room at the Emporium while staying here. I didn't hear everything, but I think he's headed into Sacramento after a day or two."

"Sounds like you heard a lot."

This time when Sadie grinned, there was a little bit of mischief showing in her expression. "How do you think I learned who you were the first day you were here?"

"As I recall, it was more like the first few hours."

She shrugged, knowing better than to deny the charge.

"He's probably at the Emporium now," she said. "He seemed pretty anxious for you to meet him."

"Yeah," Clint said as he moved in closer and slipped his hands around her waist. "That's what it says in the letter."

Sadie closed her eyes and leaned back a little so Clint could start kissing her neck. "Then don't you want to go over there?"

As he wrapped his arms around her and pressed his body against hers, Clint said, "Actually, I had something better in mind since you're here right now."

"It isn't polite to keep guests waiting."

"That's right," Clint said. "I'm your guest, so don't keep me waiting."

SIX

Sadie took slow, backward steps toward Clint's bed while still facing him. He moved right along with her, feeling her hips move under his hands while she unbuttoned her blouse to reveal a lacy, dark-blue corset. All it took was a couple of tugs to get her skirt unbuttoned and down over her hips. From there, Sadie took one step out of the discarded garment and then kicked it away.

"I hope you don't think every guest gets this kind of treatment," she whispered while peeling off Clint's shirt.

"I know they don't. Considering how much we've been getting together, there aren't enough hours in the day for you to make rounds like that."

She gave him a playful smack on the chest and then resumed undressing him. As always, she lingered for a moment at Clint's gun belt so she could let her fingers drift across the cold iron of the modified Colt. "I've barely got enough time to run the kitchen as it is."

"That's one of the things I like about you," Clint said as he buried his face in the soft curve where her neck sloped down to her shoulder. "You always smell like cake and coffee."

When she laughed, Sadie melted into his arms. The

only thing holding her up was Clint's embrace, and she allowed herself to be lowered gently onto the bed. "What else do you like about me?"

Running his palms along the front of her body, Clint savored the feel of lace and warm skin under his fingers. He managed to loosen the corset and strip it off her without too much effort. The lacy panties were next, which were the exact same shade of blue as the rest of her undergarments. "For one thing, you always match."

Clint leaned down to place his lips upon Sadie's breasts. They were just big enough to fill his hands as he cupped them. Her nipples grew hard after a bit of teasing, and became fully erect the moment he flicked his tongue over them.

While massaging her breasts and rubbing the nipples with his thumbs, Clint ran his tongue between them and felt her back arch as he kept licking all the way to the base of her neck. When he reached down to slide one hand between her legs, he could feel her dampness through the thin material of her panties.

"And when I say that you match," Clint whispered as he eased her panties off and looked down at the thatch of golden hair between her legs, "I mean that in every sense of the word."

The downy blond hair between Sadie's legs was wet enough to remind Clint of freshly poured honey. With that in mind, he moved so he could kiss a line straight down her belly and take a taste for himself.

The moment she felt his tongue glide over the lips of her pussy, Sadie grabbed hold of the back of Clint's head and pressed herself against him. She let out a soft moan as her eyes grew wide and chills started working their way under her skin.

Clint used two fingers to ease her lips apart as he teased her with his tongue. He could feel her grinding against him and guiding him with her hand. Soon, he got her trembling with excitement and pulling in a quick series of gasping breaths.

While she was still building up steam, Clint crawled on top of her and let his cock settle between her legs. Out of pure instinct, Sadie opened her legs and fitted him inside her. With one solid thrust, Clint drove all the way into her.

Sadie's pussy was already tight, but it gripped him even more as her climax drew closer. Even though her eyes were open, she seemed to be staring off into space as Clint pumped into her again and again while rubbing the sensitive skin of her clitoris.

A minute or so was all Sadie could take before she was overpowered by her orgasm. She reached out to grab hold of the bed with both hands, and nearly ripped the sheets completely off before she was able to catch her breath.

After blinking a few times, Sadie looked around as if she was trying to figure out where she was. Clint was still on top of her, looking down at her with a big smile on his face.

"You all right?" he asked.

Narrowing her eyes a bit, Sadie shoved Clint over and crawled on top of him. "I'm doing just fine," she said as she placed one hand flat upon Clint's chest and used her other hand to stroke his cock. "How about you?"

Clint leaned back and watched as she climbed on top of him. Her breasts swayed and her hair fell down over her shoulders while she looked down at him. Her hips were just big enough to give her a classic hourglass figure, not to mention a perfect place to put his hands.

"I'm doing great," he said while resting his hands on her hips and pulling her down.

Sadie bent her knees and squatted down lower. That also made it easier for her to guide him into her once more as she slowly eased herself down and took him inside her. "Is that so?" she asked. "How about now?"

Seeing her on top of him was more than enough to make

Clint's erection grow even harder. Feeling her lower onto him while he slid into her was almost too much for him to bear. She moved so slowly that Clint could feel every inch of his stiff penis being massaged by her wet lips.

When she started riding his cock at a smooth, gentle pace, Sadie knew she was practically driving Clint out of his mind. Even though she didn't hear him say anything to her, the look on Clint's face told her that well enough.

Smiling that mischievous smile of hers, Sadie lifted herself up again so she was almost standing up on the bed. She stayed that way just long enough to turn around so that she was facing the bottom half of the mattress.

Sadie lowered herself down once more as Clint scooted back so his back was propped against the headboard and he was sitting halfway up. With her new position, he could no longer see her face. But since he got a real good look at the curve of her back and the plump curves of her buttocks, Clint wasn't going to complain.

Sadie squatted once more and fitted him inside her. She then lowered herself all the way down to her knees, and then leaned back until her hair was tickling Clint's chest. Glancing over her shoulder, she looked at Clint and said, "You like the way I ride you?"

"Oh, yeah," Clint replied while sifting his fingers through her hair. "I sure do." When he felt her start to rock on him, he wrapped one arm around her middle and started pumping up into her in time to her own rhythm.

Letting out a groan, Sadie leaned forward and took hold of Clint's legs. From there, she was able to ride his cock even harder. Soon, she felt his hands on her hips, giving her subtle directions as to when she was to speed up or slow down. She followed those directions to the letter and felt Clint growing even harder inside her.

As much as Clint enjoyed watching Sadie's face when he made love to her, he also enjoyed the sight of her backside bobbing up and down on his waist. Her plump buttocks wriggled slightly when she lowered herself all the way down and were hot under the palms of his hands. Clint slapped them playfully and heard her squeal with appreciation.

"God, yes," she moaned. "Do that again."

He spanked her again, this time leaving a little red mark on her backside. Sadie responded by tossing her head back and riding him all the way to a climax that got Clint's heart slamming within his chest. When he reached around to stroke that blond pussy of hers, Clint quickly brought her to that same brink and then promptly sent her over it.

SEVEN

The Emporium was one of the finest gambling parlors frequented by Sacramento locals, but it wasn't actually inside the city of Sacramento itself. It was roughly the size of a large hotel and stuffed to brimming with tables to accommodate any and every game that could be played.

Roulette wheels were always spinning. Dice were always being tossed and cards were always being dealt. So much money changed hands inside the place that the owners of the Emporium hired their own security, which was as respected as the law and more feared than a gang of wanted killers.

Since the Emporium catered to gamblers in every way, there was food to be served at any hour and even rooms to be rented. Most of those rooms were just big enough to hold a bed, a chair, and a washbasin since the men who rented them were more concerned with their next game than the quality of their bedsprings.

Clint walked up the carpeted stairs and looked down the long row of narrow doors. When he'd first seen the room number on the letter, he'd thought it was a misprint. But there were indeed more than three dozen rooms on that

27

second floor. And it only seemed natural that the room he wanted was at the end of that row.

Henry Whiteoak never was the sort of man to make anything easy on anyone else.

Standing to one side of the little hole in the door, Clint knocked a few times and listened for a reply.

There were a few tentative steps approaching the door before the light through the peephole was blocked out.

"Who is it?" said the shaky voice from inside the room.

"It's Clint Adams."

"I can't see you."

Clint leaned to one side and waved at the little hole. Almost instantly, the latch was turned and the door was thrown open.

Henry Whiteoak stood inside with an expression on his face that was one part joy and another part petrified. "Get in here quick," he said while taking hold of the front of Clint's shirt. He started pulling Clint in, but was unable to move him.

With one hand, Clint swatted away Henry's arm and stepped inside on his own accord. "It's bad enough you make me walk all the way up these stairs and all the way down this hall, but you're going to pull me around by my shirt as well?"

"Sorry about that. I just didn't want anyone else knowing I'm here."

"Did you decide this before or after you handed out letters announcing that very thing?"

Whiteoak rolled his eyes and chuckled under his breath. "That does seem a bit odd when you put it that way. It was, however, necessary if I were to contact you with any speed. It did work, though."

"Yeah," Clint said without sharing any of Whiteoak's enthusiasm. "Now how the hell did you know I was here?"

Beaming as if he was delivering a sermon, Whiteoak said, "I try to keep track of all my good friends. After all the times you've gotten me out of hot water through the years, I want to make sure I'm there for you if you ever need assistance."

"You're a swindler and a rat, Henry. That's what put you into so much hot water in the first place."

Whiteoak's smile melted just a little. "That's a bit harsh."

"Let's see. You've cheated at cards, sold doctored tonics, peddled fraudulent claims, nearly gotten killed for pissing off the wrong people. The list goes on, and somehow I've gotten wrangled into saving your worthless hide on more than one occasion. Judging by the way you answered the door, this time isn't much better."

"This isn't like those other times," Whiteoak insisted.

Clint fixed a stare on Whiteoak that would have been enough to make nearly any poker player squirm in their seat. "So you're not on the run from someone who's trying to kill you?"

Whiteoak's smile didn't exactly fade, but it did start to resemble more of a wooden mask than anything with any real meaning. "Well, that part may still be true."

"Who is it this time?"

"That's really not the important part."

"Sure it isn't. How did you find me?"

"There's a matter of utmost urgency regarding—"

"Henry," Clint said sternly. "I asked you a question. How did you find me? And tell me more than keeping track of an old friend, because there's got to be more to it than that."

"I . . . uh . . . well . . . I sort of have associates who keep an eye out for you among others."

"Spies?" Clint asked in disbelief. "You've gone from being a lying snake-oil salesman to hiring spies to keep track of me just in case you needed your fat pulled out of the fire again?"

"Not at all! It's not half as bad as all that. We all help each other keep track of friends or other associates. It's more of a—"

"A network of spies," Clint finished. "That's just great. I feel much better now. When I read that letter, my first thought was to burn it and pretend that I never heard your name."

"But you didn't," Whiteoak pointed out. "There must be a reason for that."

"There sure is."

Hope beamed onto Whiteoak's face as if a lantern had been lit directly in front of him.

"I wanted to find out how you tracked me down so I could make sure it never happened again," Clint said. "Call off your spies before I find them, Henry, or things will become very difficult for you and every last one of them."

With that, Clint turned his back to Whiteoak and reached for the door's handle.

"A whole town may be about to be poisoned," Whiteoak quickly said.

"What?"

"I stumbled upon the evidence myself."

"And why did you need to get ahold of me before telling this to anyone?" Clint asked.

"Because it's the same town that ran me out after trying to string me up from a telegraph post."

Grudgingly, Clint turned back around.

EIGHT

Coming from anyone else, those particular words might have sounded absurd. Since they were coming from Henry Whiteoak, however, those words were just crazy enough to be true.

"I'll give you five minutes, Henry," Clint said. "The moment you try to put something over on me, I'll walk out that door. If you don't give me a good enough reason for all of this after five minutes, I'll walk out that door anyway."

"I know you haven't seen me at my finest moments over the years, but I've never done anything to cheat you, Clint. You know that."

Clint's only response to that was a few quick taps on the watch he'd taken from his pocket.

"The town's name is Piedmont," Whiteoak said. "It's a few days ride from here. Lovely little town a stone's throw from the ocean." After another couple of taps from Clint's watch, Whiteoak's speech shifted into an almost frenzied pace. "I set up shop there about a month ago. It started out as any other job. I moved in to start selling my wares."

"You mean hawk your tonics."

Whiteoak shrugged and said, "Six of one, half dozen of the other. Anyway, one of my partners became ill and needed some assistance. The town doctor had already written him off as dead when I noticed something peculiar about his symptoms.

"Sometime ago, when I was starting to ply my trade, I studied every book I could find regarding the mixing of chemicals and the creation of certain elixirs." Before Clint could get another word out, Whiteoak added, "Yes, I truly did study. Not everything I sell is sugar water, you know."

Clint nodded and motioned for Whiteoak to continue.

"The symptoms I saw reminded me of what might befall someone who had taken a dose of poorly mixed painkillers. While several different tonics are good for alleviating pain, a few are expressly mixed for that purpose." Whiteoak had to shake himself out of his sales pitch and focus on cutting to the quick.

"There are a few different mixtures that are passed around by other men in my line of work."

"You mean like recipes?" Clint asked.

"Exactly. Anyway, unlike mixing up a soup or baking a cake, things can go very wrong when dealing with some of the ingredients we use."

"Like opium, for example."

Realizing he didn't have the time to waste on defending himself, Whiteoak nodded quickly and said, "Among others, among others. The point is that some of these things can be quite dangerous if not handled properly. And before you point it out, they can be quite dangerous in any form, but that's why most men in my profession don't deal with them."

"But you still seem to know a whole lot about them," Clint pointed out.

"And you know a whole lot about guns. That doesn't necessarily make you a murderer."

Clint conceded that point with a nod.

"The symptoms I saw reminded me of something like the ones that can be caused by these particular ingredients," Whiteoak continued. "The doctor didn't catch it because they fall a bit out of his normal range of experience.

"A few days later, more people started getting sick. The only problem was that they weren't associates of mine and didn't even have any way that I know of for them to get ahold of the tonic to cause the sickness."

"You're certain it was caused by a tonic and wasn't some sort of disease or maybe a new strain of pox?"

Whiteoak scowled at Clint and shook his head. "I may not be a fully certified physician, Clint, but I know the pox when I see it. This wasn't it. Besides, my antidote worked just fine on my associate, so his ailment must have come from the source I suspected."

"I'm impressed, Henry. You actually sound like a real doctor."

Whiteoak smiled as though he was on the verge of taking a bow. "Why, thank you."

"Too bad you spend most of your time trying to figure out how to cheat your way into some money instead of earning it properly."

"I only take from those who can afford to give. Or . . . if they deserve to be taken. You probably don't know what I'm saying."

Actually, Clint had a real good handle on what Whiteoak was saying, but he wasn't about to tell him that. Instead, he asked, "Couldn't you have shared this knowledge with the doctor? Or what about the law? I'm sure they would have liked to know someone was being poisoned."

"Well, this was right around the same time that I fell out of favor with one of Piedmont's more notorious citizens. He's the owner of a saloon and very rich indeed."

"Which means he falls into your first category of victims."

"As well as the second," Whiteoak confirmed. "He's a prick by every definition of the word, and I believe he has something to do with what happened to my partner. He's just the sort to make him suffer for having anything to do

with taking a few of his dollars. I was on my way to have a
word with him when I was grabbed off the street by that
damn lynch mob."

"You think they were in on this plot too?" Clint asked.

"Honestly, no. They had . . . other grievances with me.
But Teasley sure didn't help matters. He didn't even want
to talk to me or allow me to defend myself."

"After all that happened, you still wanted to talk? I've
got to hand it to you, Henry. You've got guts, if not common sense."

"Teasley is known for offering a drink to everyone who
comes to talk business with him. Seeing as how these
chemicals are usually drunk and Teasley is the one who
would most want to see my partner dead, I'd say Teasley is
the man who is most likely to be the culprit here. I wanted
to get a drink from him as well so I could see for myself."

"Could you tell if it was poisoned?"

Reluctantly, Whiteoak nodded. "I know certain smells
and tastes to look for. It's part of my trade, after all."

"And you're certain this was poison and not just some
mistake?"

"Others have been taken ill in Piedmont and the doctor
has already shown he doesn't know how to deal with it."

"I've dealt with you enough to be suspicious, Whiteoak.
There's got to be some sort of angle here. Why the hell
would you be so concerned about people who ran you out
of town after trying to string you up?"

Whiteoak sighed and rubbed his neck as if he could still
feel that coarse rope tied around it. "I do have common
sense, Clint. Plenty of it. That's why I know those folks
were justified in being angry with me. They might have
gone too far, but that was the risk I took when I . . . plied
my trade.

"Those people don't deserve to die, however, which is
just what they'll do if more of them get poisoned. I don't
know how Teasley stumbled upon it, but that concoction he

slipped to my partner is very nasty. For that, Teasley deserves to answer for his own crime."

"And why would he poison more people?" Clint asked.

"I don't know. Perhaps he poisoned some well water to try to get to me and the others who stole from him. Perhaps it was a mistake. Either way, I can't just turn my back to it. At the very least, someone needs to go back into Piedmont to help. I'm the only one I know who knows what to do and if I show my face there again, I'll be dead in minutes.

"You can protect me," Whiteoak said. "And if Teasley is purposely poisoning people for his own ends, he's a monster that needs to be stopped before innocent folks get hurt. My time's up, Clint. Will you help me or not?"

Slowly, Clint closed his watch and put it back into his pocket. "I forgot to credit you with one more talent, Whiteoak. You're also one hell of a salesman. I'm in. But if I find out you're conning me, you'll wish to God you never even knew my name."

Whiteoak smiled and shook Clint's hand. "Partners again!"

"I must be out of my damn mind."

NINE

"What's the matter with your horse?"

Clint and Whiteoak were sitting in the driver's seat of a small wagon that had been purchased for next to nothing. The reason for that was mainly due to the fact that the wagon probably would have fallen to pieces at the sight of a rough road. As it was, the thing rattled contemptuously beneath them as if it had a mind to throw them off.

"With all that's going on, you decide to criticize my horse?" Clint asked.

Whiteoak shrugged. "Not so much of a criticism as an observation. For such a fine animal, he looks like he can barely keep his head up."

In fact, Whiteoak wasn't too far off the mark. Eclipse's big frame looked a bit odd strapped into the harness of that rickety old wagon. Although he didn't look as odd as if he were walking beside the old nag that used to pull the wagon, it was still painfully obvious that the Darley Arabian would have rather been anywhere else but where he was.

"Take a look at this contraption, for starters," Clint said. "This thing isn't much better than a pile of old wood being dragged on a sled."

"I have a perfectly good wagon that's much better than this one."

"Yeah, and it's also painted like it escaped from the circus. That's not exactly the way to sneak back into a town that wants to see you dead."

"Good point."

"I'm still thinking of a way to get you into that place without someone recognizing your face within the first few minutes."

Whiteoak waved that off with confidence. "No problem. I'll wear a disguise."

"A disguise won't do. You're a wanted man there."

"It'll do just fine. You wait and see."

Clint looked over to the man next to him just to make sure Whiteoak wasn't joking. Sure enough, the man nodded and sat up straight as if he was quoting Scripture with all the faith of a church full of preachers.

"All right," Clint said. "But you'd better not be counting on me to blast your way out of making some stupid mistake. If things go badly, I'll do what I can. If you strut in there, make a mess, and expect me to clean it up, you're in for some jail time or worse."

"Would I ask you to risk your life needlessly?"

Clint turned to fix a glare upon Whiteoak that answered that question in no uncertain terms.

"Well, I'm not asking you to do that this time," Whiteoak said.

"Good. Now tell me some more about this Teasley fellow."

"He owns the Silver Dollar Saloon and has been in business for quite a while. Most of that business comes from illicit means such as dealing in illegal goods and even having men hurt."

"He's a killer?"

"That's what I've heard," Whiteoak replied. "Of

course, there's no proof to that, but it's fairly common knowledge."

Knowing all too well how twisted some people's common knowledge could be, Clint let out a heavy sigh and flicked the reins. When he felt the leather across his back as well as the deadweight behind him, Eclipse let out a similar sigh.

"Personally, I know of at least two men he had killed," Whiteoak said.

"More common knowledge?"

"Oh, no. These are murders that Teasley himself admitted to. Granted, they were both fairly notorious cardsharps, but their bodies were found in such a state that would even turn a butcher's stomach."

"He admitted to doing that?" Clint asked.

"He bragged about it."

"All right. What else?"

"I'm pretty certain he has some political weight," Whiteoak continued. "Seeing as how Teasley can operate pretty much however he wants, that usually means he's got some connections in the right places."

"So tell me how you ran afoul of him again."

"I already told you. He caught me with my hand in the proverbial cookie jar."

Clint chuckled and said, "I want specifics. What type of game were you trying to play when you got caught?"

"There were several games actually. On one hand, my partner had come into town sometime before and got a job dealing faro. By the time I arrived, he was well established and even trusted. I ran a few crooked poker games and fleeced a few locals, but that was just to attract attention.

"The real game was being played by my partner, who started skimming off the top of his faro profits. You see, Teasley has a reputation for being a hothead, so I thought he would be so consumed by trying to catch me that he would turn his attention away from the faro games. He got so mad that he took it upon himself to play me and bust me out. That was all the opening my partner needed."

"How long did that game last?"

"An hour or so," Whiteoak replied. "But he had half his men watching me and the other half getting ready to jump on me if I went for my gun."

"Leaving your partner with free reign," Clint said.

"Exactly. He made a collection from some of the other tables to cover one big bet, which Teasley was too busy to approve, and he took the money right out the front door. Well . . . actually, it was the side door."

"Sounds like a half-brained plan."

"There's a lot more to it than that," Whiteoak said. "But that's the bare bones of it. Once my partner was on the inside, there was any number of things he could do for me as well as another partner. We even charged rent on him."

Clint looked over to Whiteoak to find him wearing a proud little smirk. "Rent?"

Whiteoak nodded. "We charged a percentage for someone to come in and take advantage of our dealer. It was like paying a small bit of change to walk away with a healthy chunk of money that was strictly profit. It's practically walking up to a cash register, helping yourself, and walking out again."

"Doesn't the house get suspicious?"

"The house just sees it as gambling losses. Besides, we make up for it by taking the money from someone else to pad the takes. There are going to be wins and losses, ups and downs. This little plan just makes sure the wins go to the right people."

"The right ones being the ones who pay the rent?"

"Exactly."

"Jesus, Henry. No wonder those folks wanted to hang you."

Still beaming with pride, Whiteoak looked stunned to

hear Clint say something that wasn't in that same vein. "It's not like I'm killing anyone."

"Do you at least see why you were run out of town?" Clint asked.

"Like I said before. Those are acceptable risks. Just like a gunfighter must accept the fact he could die any time he draws his weapon. If not for this poison nonsense, I would have licked my wounds, counted myself lucky for avoiding the noose, and moved on to the next town."

Practically every time Clint looked at Henry Whiteoak, he saw something different. Sometimes he saw a rat. Sometimes he saw a weasel. Sometimes he saw a fox, and sometimes he even saw a little nobility within those light-colored eyes.

He knew better than to trust the con man completely, but Clint did know for certain that Whiteoak was no killer. His intentions may have been skewed, but his heart was always in the right place. Even so, Clint kept his own intentions hidden behind a well-crafted mask that was unreadable by most of the top poker players in the world.

"You'd best get into your disguise, Henry. We're almost there."

TEN

Clint's warning had come a little early. Part of that was to make sure Whiteoak had enough time to pull together whatever miracle of disguise he had up his sleeve, and another reason was to give Clint some peace and quiet.

He'd ridden with Whiteoak a few times, but he always forgot just how much the man talked. Whatever moments of quiet Clint could get were well appreciated, and he knew they would be awfully rare while he and Whiteoak were together.

Whiteoak's disguise wound up being a set of old, rumpled clothes and some dirt smeared upon his face. The amazing part of it was that he truly did look like a different person with just those few aspects of his appearance altered.

Normally, Whiteoak took such great pride in his appearance that his fancy suits and starched shirts were practically part of his body. When those were removed and replaced with something so completely different, the results were startling.

"It seems like a leopard truly can change his spots," Clint said when he'd gotten his first look at Whiteoak after the disguise was in place.

41

"You think I'll be able to accompany you in the Silver Dollar?"

"Does Teasley wear thick spectacles?"

"No."

"Then I don't think you should go in that place."

"But I must!"

Already, Clint was missing the quiet he'd had while Whiteoak had been changing clothes. "Keep your head down and shut up," he snapped. "Piedmont is just ahead."

Fortunately, Whiteoak ducked down before he could see that the closest hint of the town was still about half a mile away.

"Do you still know anyone in town?" Clint asked.

Whiteoak responded in a whisper. "One of my partners should still be there. It's our common practice to stay put if one of us is run off."

"So this happens to you a lot?"

"Sometimes," Whiteoak admitted.

"Then maybe you're not as good a con man as I thought."

Even though no sound came from the wagon behind him, Clint could feel the other man prickling like a cat that just got its fur rubbed in the wrong direction.

Whiteoak was silent for the duration of the ride.

Eclipse pulled the wagon grudgingly, but without much of a fuss. All things considered, Clint hated strapping Eclipse to that rickety pile of wood more than anything else so far.

"Don't worry, boy," he said. "We'll go for a nice run before too long."

Whether or not Eclipse heard or understood that, it didn't seem to matter. He was still pulling that junk heap of a wagon, so he was still not a happy fellow.

The town of Piedmont was actually very inviting. Its streets were well maintained. The boardwalks on either side of the streets appeared to be relatively straight. Even the people Clint saw were well dressed and fairly cosmopolitan. Considering how close they were to the Pacific and the trade routes that sailed on that ocean, it wasn't too much of a surprise that the latest fashions were on display.

Even the air felt refreshing, since it smelled of the ocean. Clint couldn't see that wide expense of salt water, but the winds were strong enough to give his nose a healthy sample. By the time he turned onto Main Street, he was wearing a smile that he didn't have to fake. Even Eclipse was walking a little easier. Of course, he'd picked up speed as soon as he spotted the large double doors of a nearby stable.

The occasional eye would be turned to the back of Clint's wagon, but all those people saw was a dirty figure slumped against the sideboard with a floppy hat pulled over his eyes. Although there wasn't a single suspicious glare among the locals, their glances were enough to keep Whiteoak perfectly quiet and perfectly still.

When Clint saw his first glimpse of the Silver Dollar Saloon, he got a taste of what it must feel like for Whiteoak and his partners to walk up to a place knowing you're going to pick it clean. Clint felt nervous and excited at the same time, as though the saloon was a pretty girl and Clint was nervously approaching her.

Behind him, Whiteoak grunted, "I think I'm going to be sick."

It seemed the romance was over for him.

ELEVEN

Clint stepped into the Silver Dollar and pulled in a long breath. Even though it had been an hour or so since he'd passed it by that first time, he still felt that rumble in his belly that had nothing at all to do with being hungry. Eclipse was in a comfortable stall and Whiteoak was tucked away in a hotel room, which left Clint free to move about without hindrance.

"Howdy, stranger," came a deep, scratchy voice from the end of the bar.

When Clint looked over there, he saw a stout man with thick, dark hair that appeared to have been greased to his scalp. A waxed mustache tapered into points, which barely even moved as the face it was on shifted into a wide smile.

"Welcome to the Silver Dollar. What can I do for you?"

"You have any faro tables around here?" Clint asked.

The man walked around the bar without taking his eyes off Clint. It reminded Clint of a wolf making its way through thick brush toward its prey.

"You want to buck the tiger, huh?" the man asked. "Ever think about trying your hand at craps? We just got a table put in the other day."

"Faro's more my game."

"Well, we're between dealers right now and before you ask, we ain't looking for a new one."

"What happened to the last dealer?"

The man reached back with one hand to snap his fingers. Less than a second later, the bartender slapped an empty mason jar into the man's waiting hand. When the man brought the jar around for Clint to see, he shook it up a bit for effect.

The jar wasn't exactly empty. There were several white objects rattling around in there that were slightly smaller than dice. Upon closer examination, Clint saw they were teeth. Fresh teeth, judging by the color of the blood at some of their roots.

"The last dealer was a goddamn cheat," the man with the jar said. "And this is the only part of a cheater that spends much time in my place."

"Those all his teeth?" Clint asked.

"Nope. There have been other contributors in the past, but the list gets shorter as this jar gets fuller. Know what I mean, friend?"

Clint forced a smile onto his face and nodded.

"So, even though we ain't got a faro game going at the moment, you can rest assured whatever games you play in the Dollar are above board. By the way," the man added as he gave the jar back and offered his hand to Clint, "my name's Cal Teasley. I own this establishment."

"Pleased to meet you."

Teasley kept hold of Clint's hand even after shaking it. "No need to be so modest, Mr. Adams. You can introduce yourself."

"Seems like I don't have to."

"Actually, no. I recognized that face the moment you stepped through that door."

"I hope it's not because of anything I have to apologize for," Clint said with a grin.

"Not at all! Any saloon owner worth his salt should be

able to spot a man like you. It makes for good business while you're here, and even after you leave." Leaning in close, Teasley dropped his voice a bit and nudged Clint with his elbow as he added, "Some of these chowder heads will pay extra money to have a drink in the same spot you were standing."

"Is that a fact?"

"It is, sir. Perhaps you should think about opening your own saloon."

"Actually, I was thinking of a friend of mine in West Texas who owns one. I wonder if he charges for spots like that."

"If he does, don't hold it against him. Every saloon owner's got to hustle if his place is gonna stand out from all the others out there. And just to show my heart's in the right place, your drinks are on me so long as you're drinking here."

"Can't have your main attraction finding another watering hole?"

"Nothing of the sort, but if you do some gambling here as well, I'll toss in free meals as well."

"That could be a mistake," Clint warned. "I eat a lot of steak."

Teasley grinned and snapped his fingers once more. "Cook up a steak for my friend Clint Adams here."

The barkeep nodded and looked over at Clint.

"Medium well should be fine," Clint said, which got a nod from the barkeep as the smaller fellow headed into another room.

Although it went against every instinct Clint had to announce his presence like that, it was more or less a part of the plan he and Whiteoak had discussed on the final leg of their ride into town. Besides, it wasn't as if there was much Clint could have done to stop Teasley from spotting Clint and marking him for all of his customers.

"I hear poker's more your game, Mr. Adams. Or should I call you Clint?"

"Either one's fine for now," Clint replied. "As for the games, I guess I could be tempted into a few hands of five-card."

"Any preference as to the stakes?"

"I just got into town, Teasley. Let me have my meal before I get picked clean and tossed out."

Teasley laughed and slapped Clint on the shoulder. Somehow, he managed to keep his spirit high and his expression good-natured when he said, "If I didn't want you around, you would have been tossed out before taking two steps in here."

"You think so?" Clint asked.

Even though there wasn't a bit of menace in Clint's voice, Teasley flinched just a bit when he heard those words. And even though Clint didn't make a single move toward his gun, plenty of eyes darted toward the modified Colt at his side.

"No need to get our blood boiling," Clint said with a wide grin. "Poker will do just fine."

Teasley grinned with a mixture of victory and relief. "You heard the man! He wants a game. Someone deal him in!"

TWELVE

Whiteoak was supposed to stay put. Before Clint had left the hotel room, he specifically ordered Whiteoak to stay in the room and get some sleep. But Whiteoak knew that Clint wasn't concerned with how much sleep he got or how well rested he was. Clint was worried that things might get botched up again.

If he was going to work with Clint as an equal partner, Whiteoak knew he couldn't let Clint think such terrible things about him. Since Clint's doubts weren't exactly unwarranted, Whiteoak decided to put his partner's mind at ease the only way possible.

He needed to prove himself.

Using the small oval mirror nailed to the wall, Whiteoak touched up the carefully smeared dirt upon his face. He smiled proudly at the result, confident in the knowledge that nobody in town would give him a second glance.

He resisted the urge to straighten his rumpled jacket before leaving the room. Not only would that have ruined the effect of his disguise, but it would have made the gun at his hip that much easier to spot. Whiteoak never had much of a gun hand, but he knew how to protect himself when push came to shove.

"All right," he said to his reflection. "Time to see just how good an actor I truly am."

Opening the door, Whiteoak took a quick look outside to see if anyone was in the hallway. The coast was clear, so he stepped outside and hurried down the short flight of stairs leading to the front door. Even though he made it out safely, just being in the streets of Piedmont by himself was enough to send a chill down his spine.

The last time he'd seen those streets was when he'd been standing on top of those crates. Just thinking about it was enough to make his breath catch in the back of his throat. Whiteoak did his best to shake free of those thoughts, and pulled in a few deep breaths. He kept his head down and walked to a little sewing shop a few blocks away.

Every time he saw someone looking his way, Whiteoak's hand flinched toward his gun. The weapon stayed in its holster during the entire length of his walk. When he got to the small storefront, Whiteoak stopped and looked into the front window.

A small, elderly woman waved at him from inside. Her second wave was more of a shooing motion to discourage him before he even thought about coming inside. Whiteoak waved back to her, playing up the part of filthy drunk as much as his acting abilities would allow. Once he saw the woman walk up to the window and pull the curtains over it, he knew he was doing a passable job.

"You need to learn to get along better with the locals," came a voice from Whiteoak's right.

Recognizing the voice immediately, Whiteoak purposely turned his back to the speaker as if he was looking at something across the street. "You have any troubles since I left?" Whiteoak asked in a whisper.

There was a slight pause as someone walked from one storefront to another on the other side of the street. Even though that person didn't seem the least bit interested in what was going on, Whiteoak and the other person kept quiet until there was nobody in sight.

"You joking?" the voice asked once the coast was clear. "This town couldn't talk about anything else once you took off running. The only way to make a better distraction would be to set the church on fire."

"I did not take off running," Whiteoak corrected. Even though he still refused to make eye contact with the other person, he straightened up as though he was addressing a committee. "I made a daring escape, collected my wagon, and made a strategic retreat."

"Whatever you call it, you gave me more than enough breathing room."

"You been able to find out anything?"

"Yeah. There's more sick folks at the doctor's office. They're not as bad as Josh was, but they're getting there."

"Did they drink at the Silver Dollar?"

"Yep."

Whiteoak looked at the ground and heard voices coming from down the street. A group of people were turning the corner and would be looking his way at any moment. Another few locals were stepping out of a different shop and had their eye on the sewing shop.

"Keep an eye on the hotel," Whiteoak said. "And see what else you can find before we talk again."

"Did you bring any help? Since Teasley is getting jumpy, we're going to need some backup."

"I got help," Whiteoak said as he began stumbling down the boardwalk. "Just do your part and we'll do ours."

Whiteoak felt his heart jump into his throat when one of the folks walking toward the sewing shop looked at him with more than a passing glance. The silver-haired woman peered at him through wire-rimmed spectacles and squinted as if committing every line of his face to memory.

With every second that dragged by, he imagined the old lady recognizing him and then screaming for help.

He pictured lawmen swarming in from all sides to snatch him up and drag him off to jail.

Or worse yet, he imagined any number of men who'd put that noose around his neck storming in so they could finish the job.

At least one of Teasley's men would be in that group to make certain Whiteoak didn't pull another miracle from up his sleeve. That train of thought made Whiteoak imagine the bite of his own straight-edge as it was raked across his throat.

"Filthy vagrant," the old lady sneered as she turned up her nose and quickened her pace into the sewing shop.

Whiteoak let out a breath and pulled his hat down to cover even more of his face. Although he tried to uphold his drunk act, he was one of the fastest drunks to ever find his way into a hotel room.

THIRTEEN

Clint excused himself the moment his steak was ready. Although he'd walked to one of the back tables so he could enjoy his meal, he wasn't about to eat anything served in a place he thought might be poisoning people. Instead, he looked for another door out of the place and left through it as quickly as possible.

The meal smelled good enough to make his stomach rumble, but he somehow managed to keep from taking a single bite. As soon as he stepped into public view, Clint felt like an absolute idiot for walking around with a plate in one hand and a glass in the other. His only other alternative was to fill his pockets with food and drink, and as ridiculous as that sounded, he quickly thought that was the way he should have gone.

Instead, he simply kept his chin up and a smile on his face. Clint walked down the street and into his hotel as if carrying his supper around was the most natural thing in the world. Since the looks he got weren't too perplexed, he thought he'd pulled off his act fairly well.

"You delivering that to one of the guests?" the clerk at the hotel's front desk asked.

Clint nodded and gave his room number.

"I can take that up for you if you like," the clerk offered.

Clint shook his head and headed for the room. "No need. I know the way."

Like most other folks Clint ran into along the way, the clerk seemed more than happy to forget about what he'd seen and get on with his own business.

"I brought something for you," Clint announced after unlocking the door and pushing it open. When he stepped inside, however, he quickly realized that there was nobody in that room to hear him.

"Henry?" Setting down the plate and glass, Clint took another look around the room as his hand drifted toward the Colt holstered at his hip. Since the room was fairly small and sparsely furnished, that second look didn't take much longer than the first.

Just to be certain he covered every possibility, Clint even squatted down to look under the bed. Once he was satisfied that Henry was truly not in the room, Clint felt his blood start to heat up.

"Goddammit, Henry," Clint muttered to himself. "How hard is it to follow simple directions?"

When Clint stomped out of the room, he slammed the door so hard behind him that he could hear the plate and glass rattle on the table where he'd left them.

Clint walked through the lobby and out the hotel without getting so much as a glance from the clerk. Once he stepped outside, however, he stopped and looked around as a realization settled into his mind: If Whiteoak was missing or had just wandered off, Clint didn't have the first notion of where to look for him.

Standing on the side of the street, Clint sifted through all he could remember about when Whiteoak had been prattling on during their ride into town. There had been plenty of things said, but not one of them gave him a clue as to where Whiteoak would go when he got the chance.

The plan was for Whiteoak to stay put, rest up, and

then try to get in touch with whatever partners of his were
still in town. More than once, Clint had tried to get some
more information out of Whiteoak regarding those partners, but that seemed to be one of the con man's most
guarded secrets.

Clint shook his head and cursed under his breath for going along with Whiteoak on yet another wild-goose chase.
In fact, he couldn't think of a good reason why he hadn't
handed the con man over to the law on any of the other oc-
casions when they'd crossed paths.

Until something better came to mind, Clint decided to
just stick to the plan he'd formulated for himself. He hadn't
been away from the Silver Dollar for long, but surely Clint
would be missed before too much longer. That is, unless
Teasley had already started looking by now.

Clint nearly had the scowl wiped off his face when he
rounded the corner and was in sight of the Dollar once
more. Then again, it had taken so much effort to stop won-
dering where the hell Whiteoak had gone that he didn't see
the incoming fist until it was less than an inch from his
face.

Reflexively, Clint pivoted back and to one side so he
could avoid the blow. But the effort came a bit too late and
he caught a good portion of knuckles across his chin. In
fact, since the punch didn't land squarely, it stung that
much more.

While Clint tried to shake out the fog that had rolled
into his head, he saw a wide, gnarled face leering at him.
The man was as big as he was ugly, and smiled at Clint
with a gap-toothed grin.

"It ain't polite to eat and run, boy," the big man said.

FOURTEEN

"Who are you?" Clint asked after shaking off the effects of that first punch.

For a man his size, the big fellow moved like a bullet. He lunged forward with his grin still intact, swinging an arm that was as thick as a tree trunk. Even though he missed with that punch, another followed soon after it, connecting with Clint solidly in his chest.

"I'm the one that's beating the hell out of you," the man grunted.

That punch to his chest rattled Clint right down to his boots. Some parts of his brain were still scrambled as he launched himself into motion. Luckily, they weren't the parts that he needed to lash out with a few quick strikes of his own.

Clint's left fist caught the man in the ribs, and then his right fist slammed into the middle of his torso. From his own experience, Clint knew all too well how being hit in that spot not only took the wind out of a man's lungs, but also dimmed the light in his eyes for a while.

The big man paused for a second to catch his breath, but recovered in a fraction of the time Clint had hoped he'd bought for himself.

Like a narrow branch that had been bent back and re-
leased, the big man's arm snapped out with a quick backhanded swing. Clint's survival instinct alone got him
down quick enough to avoid getting his head knocked off
his shoulders. The big man's arm hacked through the air
over Clint's head with the sound of a club being swung by
a giant.

While he was down there, Clint didn't waste a single moment. He busied himself by hitting the big man in the stomach three quick times in the same spot. By the time the third
blow had landed, Clint could hear labored breathing coming
from over his head.

Clint looked up, saw the big man glaring down at him,
and took another opportunity to end the fight then and
there. He clasped both fists together and stood up while
bringing both arms straight up as well. With a motion that
was similar to uprooting a tree, Clint swung his arms up
and connected with the big man's chin.

Wearing a surprised look on his face, the big man
reared up and bent back as blood spewed from his nose.
His arms extended to either side as his hands opened in
search of something to grab onto. Finding nothing but air,
the big man staggered back and quickly lost his balance at
the edge of the boardwalk.

Clint was still feeling the sting of the glancing blows
he'd taken as he reached out to gently push the big man
over the edge and into the street. Even as he heard the man
hit the dirt, Clint was looking around to see who would be
the next one to try and jump him.

All he saw were a few astonished locals with their eyes
wide and their jaws hanging open. The instant they saw
Clint looking their way, those people turned around and
hurried off to wherever they'd been going in the first place.

Clint's eyes were fixed upon the Silver Dollar, and he
crossed the street to head straight into the saloon. He didn't
take two steps before he was stopped by a viselike grip that

clamped around his ankle and started crushing the bones of his leg.

"Where you goin', boy?" the big man with the gaps in his teeth growled. "We ain't through yet."

The big man kept hold of Clint's ankle as he got his legs beneath him and started climbing to his feet. He even kept his grip intact as Clint started kicking and fighting to get his leg free. All that did was make it that much harder for Clint to keep his balance as the big man stood up.

Feeling as if he was trying to stand up while the ground was slowly tilted beneath him, Clint was forced to use both arms to steady himself before he fell over. By the time the bigger man was up, Clint was flapping his arms and hopping on one leg to keep from landing on his back.

The big man's ugly face split open into a bloody grin as he watched Clint dance in front of him. With the flip of his wrist, he sent Clint sprawling to the dirt and then lumbered after him.

"I'm gonna stomp yer head like a grape," the big man announced as he lifted his leg and started to follow up on his words.

Clint was able to roll to one side just as the man's boot pounded into the ground next to him. The impact was so hard that he could feel it rumble through the earth and shake his bones. When he saw another boot dropping onto him, Clint kept right on rolling as a second impact jarred the street.

Although he never drew his gun unless it was absolutely necessary, Clint was out of options when it came to stopping the big man's assault. He might have landed a few punches, but they did as much damage as a tuft of straw swatting against a side of beef.

The Colt filled Clint's hand after a quick flicker of motion from his right arm. Its weight gave Clint a healthy dose of confidence that he would walk away from the scuffle without getting his limbs torn from their sockets.

That confidence lasted right up until the big man reached out and swatted away the gun as though he was relieving a child of his toy.

"That ain't fair," the big man said. "Now you gone and made me angry."

Clint's gun was still sailing through the air when he scurried off to catch it. After crawling a few quick steps, Clint launched himself off both feet and extended his arms so he could reach with both hands. Just when he thought he hadn't pushed off hard enough, Clint felt the Colt land in his left palm like a gift from above.

Twisting at the waist, Clint shifted onto one knee so he could sight along the barrel of his gun at the big man. As soon as he got the bruiser in his sights, Clint heard something else rumbling toward him. Instead of some giant trying to take him apart, the source of this rumbling was a stagecoach rolling down the street, heading straight for Clint.

Before the stagecoach could run him over, Clint pushed back again and launched into an awkward, backward roll. He came to a stop when his back knocked against the boardwalk on the opposite side of the street and the wagon rolled by amid the thunder of heavy wheels and clomping hooves.

It took Clint less than a second to find his target again and take aim.

The big man was still grinning when he raised both hands, turned around, and calmly walked away.

FIFTEEN

Clint was deciding whether or not he wanted to chase after the big man when someone else caught his attention. Since he was still feeling the punches he'd taken and his blood was still racing through his veins, Clint's first impulse was to keep the Colt up and ready when he turned to see who else was coming at him.

When he saw the badge on the man's chest, however, Clint holstered his gun.

"What's the meaning of all this?" the lawman asked.

Clint shook his head and kept his hands well away from his gun. Before he could respond to the question, the lawman was standing directly in front of him and glaring straight into his eyes.

"Did you start a fight out here?" the lawman asked. "Am I gonna have to take that gun away and toss you into a cell?"

"I didn't start anything," Clint said. "I didn't even fire a shot."

Slowly, the lawman started to nod. "All right then. Just be sure that you watch yourself around here."

With that, the lawman turned and walked away while encouraging the bystanders to do the same.

Clint watched the lawman as if he couldn't believe what he was seeing. He didn't know whether he should be grateful to be done with the confrontation before any more trouble came his way, or be angry that the best the law could do was throw some cross words at the wrong man.

Deciding to put all of that aside for the moment, Clint headed to the Silver Dollar. When he walked into the saloon, everything was just as he'd left it. The only difference was that a skinny man was now playing a banjo in one corner while stomping his feet to the rhythm.

"There you are," Teasley said. "I was just about to form a search party. You prefer to eat in the fresh air or did Bob's face put you off your food?"

The barkeep, who must have been Bob, grumbled a few choice words at Teasley's back before continuing to wipe off the tables.

While keeping himself from looking too aggressive, Clint walked up to Teasley and stared him dead in the eye. "Do you know a man about half a foot taller than me with arms like logs and a face uglier than a half-eaten carcass?"

"Sounds like a few customers I've seen. Why?" Suddenly, Teasley squinted and took a closer look at Clint's face. "What the hell happened to you?"

"Someone tried to knock my head off just outside your place."

"That fella you just described?"

Clint nodded.

"Son of a bitch! I hope you took good care of him, Clint. Jesus, if I would'a known that was going on, I would have come out to help. I didn't even hear a gunshot."

"There wasn't any gunshot," Clint replied as he watched Teasley's face for any trace of a lie. What perplexed him the most was that there wasn't so much as a flicker in the man's expression when he talked or even when he listened.

"So what happened?" Teasley asked. "Was he some

drunk you saw in here? Because if he is, I may know the bastard's name."

"He wasn't drunk."

"Well, then, he might be new in town, because he sure doesn't sound familiar."

There it was.

Right when Teasley said that last part, Clint saw something on the man's face that was like a single muscle that didn't quite fall in line with the rest. Years of playing poker had sharpened Clint's senses to a razor's edge when it came to looking for signals like that.

Teasley was lying. At least, he was lying about that last thing he'd said.

"Why don't you play some poker?" Teasley said. "I've got some players lined up that will give you one hell of a game."

The saloon owner wasn't lying about that.

When Clint sat down at the chair Teasley offered, he saw a wide range of faces at the table with him. As far as poker players went, they ran the gamut from good to bad, while hitting every spot in between. Then, just before one of them was busted out, he made a miraculous comeback, which didn't surprise Clint in the least.

After less than two hours of playing, Clint stood up and excused himself from the table.

In a matter of seconds, Teasley was rushing over to him. "What's the matter? You can't be done already."

"I just got into town, Teasley. My food's settling and I'd like some rest. Don't get your pants in a bunch. I'll be back here before you know it."

"Maybe you just need something to drink. You know, to wash down that steak. You haven't had one drink the whole time you were here, so you gotta be thirsty."

"I'll be back in a while," Clint repeated. "See you then."

There was no mistaking the finality in Clint's voice, so

Teasley held back the next round of coaxing that was about to come out of his mouth. Instead, he plastered on a smile, nodded, and said, "Long as I can count on you coming back."

"You can. Thanks for the hospitality." With that, Clint tipped his hat, cashed in his chips, and left.

Teasley's smile barely lasted for the amount of time it took for the front door to swing shut. He turned around and leaned against the bar until one of his men sauntered up to stand next to him. The man was tall, burly, and had long, black hair hanging in greasy strands from beneath a dented bowler hat.

"You want me to get him back?" the man asked.

"Nah. He ain't some dude we can muscle until he loses his wad at the table. Besides, that's not what I want him to do. He's an attraction, Mike. Having a man like him around here will make more folks want to stop by and hear the stories about him."

"What if he don't come back?"

Teasley waved that off like a gnat that had been buzzing around his head. "Did you see where he went when he left here?"

Mike squinted and looked at the door as if Clint was standing there with the answer Teasley wanted to hear. "What're you talking about?"

"When Adams left," Teasley snarled. "You know! When he walked out of here with his food and drink. Didn't you keep on him to see what he was doing?"

"I figured he was eating, Cal."

"Eating?"

Once again, Mike looked around as if someone else would give him some assurance. But the ones in the bar who didn't know them were too busy with their own troubles, and the ones who did were smart enough to stay away when Teasley took on that tone of voice.

"I pay you to do what I say and I said for you to keep an

eye on Adams," Teasley snarled. "He could have taken his steak to eat in the sheriff's office while offering his services for all we know!"

"The sheriff ain't a concern, Cal."

"He could be if he thinks he can get a man like The Gunsmith on his side. Now pull your head out of your ass and do your job!"

"All right," Mike said sheepishly. "Sorry about that."

After a few quiet moments, Teasley smacked Mike on the back of the head. "I said do your job!"

Gritting his teeth, Mike strode out the front door and started looking around to see which direction Clint had gone.

SIXTEEN

Clint wasn't exactly running back to his hotel, but he had enough steam in his strides that he made the walk there in record time. Even so, to him it felt as if the trip took triple the amount of time simply because he was watching every angle as best he could every step of the way.

The last time he'd been taking a casual walk, he'd almost gotten his teeth knocked out of his head. The next time he met up with that beast, Clint knew the big man wasn't going to be so gentle. Fortunately, that big man didn't seem to be up for another round just yet, because Clint made it to the hotel without getting ambushed a second time.

He fit the key into the lock, turned it, and opened the door in one smooth series of motions. Although he'd made this trip without incident, Clint didn't feel like pressing his luck and staying out in the open for longer than necessary. The room might have been safe, but it wasn't exactly empty.

Henry Whiteoak sat on the edge of the bed, hunched over the plate of food Clint had left in the room a few hours ago. He gripped a fork in one hand and the glass Clint had left in the other. When he looked up at Clint, he started to say hello, but only got out a few garbled grunts.

Clint stepped inside and calmly shut the door.

After settling down into a chair, he took a few seconds to watch Whiteoak try to gulp down the food he was chewing so he might be able to talk.

"Enjoying the steak?" Clint asked.

Whiteoak nodded and smiled.

"Not too cold for you?"

After holding up a finger, Whiteoak finished chewing, swallowed his mouthful, and shrugged. "I would have preferred it to be a little warmer, but I appreciate the gesture all the same. After all, it's my fault for not being here when you brought it up."

Clint nodded. "You feeling all right?"

"Yes. Why?"

"Because that food came from the Silver Dollar."

Freezing with another hunk of steak on his fork and halfway to his mouth, Whiteoak dropped the plate and started to lift the glass.

"So did the water," Clint added.

Even though Whiteoak had already drained half the water before Clint had gotten there, it was his first instinct to send the sip he'd just taken into the air in a loud spray.

Clint was able to keep a straight face for about a second before he cracked up and laughed wholeheartedly.

"I'm glad you think that's funny," Whiteoak said as he brushed the bits of food off himself and started dabbing at the water on his face. "Is that really true?"

"Yes."

Whiteoak turned white as a sheet. "I could be poisoned!"

"Stop being a baby. If there was truly something wrong with that food, you would have felt it by now."

"Then why did you bring it up here? Wasn't it so I could check it out and see if it had been tampered with?"

"Partially. I was actually going to take my chances and have my food in some peace and quiet. Teasley may not have reason to kill me just yet, but he can sure be a pest when a man's just trying to have some food and a few moments to himself."

Clint chuckled again and took the plate away from Whiteoak. "Damn. You sure get cranky when you mess up your clothes. I can only imagine what would happen if you were wearing one of those fancy suits."

"It wouldn't be pretty, I can assure you."

There wasn't much left on the plate besides one last hunk of steak, so Clint picked it up and popped it in his mouth. Since that was all there was, he was hoping the meat wouldn't be worth the fuss. Unfortunately, it was delicious and Clint's stomach growled for more.

"Where the hell were you, by the way?" Clint asked.

"When was that?"

"You know damn well what I'm talking about. You were supposed to stay here and when I came by to drop this off, you were gone. Where did you go?"

"I just wanted to get a jump on what we discussed earlier."

"You mean checking to see if your partners were still watching that meeting spot?"

Whiteoak nodded and finished up the last of his repairs to his clothes. Although the shirt looked just as rumpled and dirty as it had when he'd started, he somehow liked what he saw better now that he'd fussed with it for a while.

"I went there and had a nice little chat," Whiteoak reported. "Seems that, even though you escaped it, other folks are getting sick."

"Anyone you know?"

"I'm not sure. My partner has been laying low, so I thought one of us could go and check in on the situation for ourselves." When he said that, Whiteoak glanced intently at Clint.

"Fine, I'll go see what I can find at the doctor's office,"

Clint said. "But I'm getting something to eat first and you're staying put."

Whiteoak held up his hand and made a silent vow. For some reason, that didn't strike Clint as being particularly valuable.

SEVENTEEN

After a little bit of asking around, Clint found out where to find the town's doctor. The office was a few streets down in a quieter section of Piedmont that had a good view of the creek that ran along the outskirts of town. As Clint walked to the office, he could hear the turning of some sort of wheel in a mill built alongside the water.

Clint walked up to the front door, knocked once, and realized the door was already open. He pushed it open the rest of the way and stepped inside.

"Hello?" Clint said.

He was quickly greeted by a nurse wearing a white apron, her hair tied back by a bandanna. "Yes? Can I help you?"

"I was hoping to have a word with the doctor."

"Dr. Chase is busy right now. Are you feeling ill?"

"No. I just wanted to ask a few questions."

"Are you a reporter?"

Clint flinched at the tone in her voice, which sounded as irritated as it did suspicious. "No. Have you been getting a lot of reporters through here?"

The nurse let out a sigh after looking Clint over carefully. It seemed that she liked what she saw because she seemed noticeably less irritated when she spoke again. "With this strange sickness going around, there have been plenty of folks stopping by to ask their questions. Usually, it's only the reporters who are gruesome enough and tenacious enough to come skulking around under those circumstances."

"I'm not a reporter. My name is Clint Adams. A friend of mine told me about this disease and I wanted to see how widespread it was."

"Is your friend one of the infected?"

"No, but he lost someone to it not too long ago."

"Really? What was his name?"

Clint paused and tried to think about how he should continue. On one hand, telling the truth could very well destroy what little advantage he and Whiteoak had for keeping their heads low. On the other hand, the nurse had an edge to her that made Clint certain she would shut up tight the moment she knew she was being lied to.

"It was a friend of Henry Whiteoak," Clint said. "I believe he passed on a week or two ago."

Surprisingly enough, the nurse didn't scowl at the mention of Whiteoak's name. So far, that put her one up on most people Clint encountered who'd crossed paths with the con man.

"Oh, you must be talking about Joshua. He mentioned your friend's name once or twice before he died. I think Mr. Whiteoak even came by to visit him. Wasn't he in some trouble with the law?"

After giving silent thanks for the fact that not everyone in a town kept up on the seedier happenings, Clint nodded and said, "There was a bit of trouble, yes. I'm more interested in knowing what happened to Josh. Since there was that trouble with Mr. Whiteoak, I doubt anyone will be able to tell Josh's family what happened."

The nurse's eyes took on a warm glow as her posture relaxed. She even took a step toward Clint and patted his hand. "That's very kind of you, Mr. Adams. After having so many people just being concerned for themselves, it does me good to see someone thinking of others."

Although Clint hadn't thought about Josh's family until just then, he suddenly felt bad for not doing so. The instant he saw the warm glow on the nurse's face, he resolved to make certain he wasn't just feeding her a line.

"Come in," the nurse said as she turned and waved for Clint to follow. "Don't worry about the other patients. As near as we've been able to tell, they're not suffering from anything infectious."

"Are you certain of that?"

"Unless it's something very new or very exotic. In which case, the odds are that it's too late to do anything about it anyway."

"You sound like you know a lot about this sort of thing."

The nurse had taken Clint down a narrow hallway and into a room that wasn't much more than a place to hang coats. She stooped down so she could remove a small wooden bin from beneath a footboard and started sifting through it. "You mean the doctor knows," she said.

"No," Clint said. "I mean you. I'll bet the doctor knows a thing or two as well."

When she looked up at him, she grinned. "Most folks assume I know a lot about changing bed linens and feeling foreheads. I did serve a good amount of time at a clinic in New York City."

"Why so far from home?"

"I was far from home when I was in New York, and that was so I could go to school. I probably shouldn't have come home if I wanted anything close to my own practice, but Dr. Chase seems to appreciate me."

"I'll bet he does," Clint said. With a wink, he added, "It's always good to have someone around who knows what they're doing."

The nurse caught herself laughing, and then stopped it right away. While glancing nervously toward the larger neighboring room where the patients were resting, she stood up and handed a small bundle to Clint. "Here you go. These are Joshua's things. Since he's gone and Mr. Whiteoak won't be coming back, it should be safe to hand them over to you. Do you know where to send them?"

"I know just who to ask."

"Good. Bless you, Mr. Adams, for aiding this poor soul's family."

"I don't believe I got your name."

"It's Dorothy."

"I'm obliged for all your help, Dorothy. By the way, you mentioned others coming around asking about these patients."

She scowled slightly and nodded. "I could tell they were fishing for information or just trying to get a look at what's going on in here. I'm amazed at how many ghoulish sorts come by just so they can see the misfortune of others."

"Probably just curious," Clint said. "Especially since a sickness could mean a lot of people might get hurt or even die."

"And a bunch of gawkers coming around and then spreading their rumors won't do anything but start a panic," Dorothy shot back with a tone in her voice that also gave a very clear warning to Clint that she meant business. "As soon as we know what it is or how to treat it, we'll tell the newspaper ourselves."

After taking a breath and looking at the little bundle in Clint's hands, Dorothy put a professional smile onto her face and said, "I know you wouldn't take part in such a thing as that, Mr. Adams. I saw that much in your eyes. Otherwise, you never would have made it in here."

The funny part was that her words held more weight in Clint's mind than the similar threat Teasley had made not too long ago regarding cheaters being tossed out of the Silver Dollar. "I have no doubt about that, ma'am," Clint said with a deferential nod. "But if I do have any questions regarding this situation, would you mind if I came to get your expert opinion on the matter?"

Dorothy nodded. "I'd be glad to help if I can, Mr. Adams."

"You've already done plenty. Thanks for your time."

On his way out, Clint glanced at the patients lying in the larger room filled with cots and tables. Although he was no doctor, Clint could tell that they weren't in good shape. In fact, more than one of them looked like they were about to meet their maker. At that particular moment, Clint couldn't have felt more useless.

EIGHTEEN

When he walked out of the doctor's office, Clint felt terrible for even considering going through Josh's things. Even so, if there was a chance that something in there could be useful, he also had an obligation to take a look. But with that in mind, Clint still had no trouble picturing Dorothy's stern, disapproving glare.

Before he had a chance to think about it any further, Clint spotted a familiar face from the corner of his eye. He couldn't put a name to that face, but he did know the last time he'd seen it was at the Silver Dollar.

Clint didn't look directly at the man who was shadowing him across the street, but he did keep a careful watch on where the man walked and how quickly he moved.

It didn't take long for Clint to realize that the man was most definitely following him. Every turn Clint took, the man stayed right with him. Whenever Clint picked up speed or slowed down, the man kept pace. But when Clint finally rounded a corner and stopped to see how long it took for the man to arrive, the other fellow never appeared.

Clint stood there for a few moments before he began to suspect something had happened. The longer he waited, however, the more convinced he became that the man was no longer playing their game of follow the leader.

That meant Clint had either lost him or the man had gotten what he needed and headed back to the saloon.

Before Clint could head back in the direction he'd really wanted to go, he saw someone round the very corner he was watching and grab his attention. Granted, the brunette had a dark sensuality about her even though she was dressed in a simple pair of jeans and a dark red shirt, but that wasn't what had caught Clint's eye.

She'd waved at him.

It wasn't just a simple how-do-you-do, but a gesture intended to grab his eye and keep it on her. The next move she made was to point toward a small general store not far from where Clint was standing.

Since it was too late to pretend he hadn't seen her, Clint headed for the store while keeping her in his sight. Of course, the seductive motion of her hips as she headed for that same store might have been enough to draw him in no matter what.

"I hope that wave was meant for me," Clint said as he came up beside the brunette. "Because if it wasn't, this is a little embarrassing."

"It was meant for you, Adams," she said slyly. "I thought you might want to thank me."

Since he was obviously meant to be surprised by the fact that she knew his name, Clint kept his expression neutral and his voice level. "Thank you for what?"

"For diverting that ape who was on your tail."

Clint dropped his casual act and turned to take one more look at the corner. There was still no trace of the big man he'd spotted a few minutes before.

"He wasn't as big as that one who beat you to a pulp," she said, "but he looked like an ape to me."

"All right," Clint said. "Who are you?"

Smiling victoriously, the brunette turned so her shoulders were squared to him and she held out her hand. Her hair was thick and a few inches longer than shoulder length, with streaks of lighter brown running through the black. Her skin was lightly tanned, and her eyes held a playful craftiness that came only after a woman learned to harness the power God had given her.

Her jeans hugged a set of smoothly rounded hips. She wore her shirt buttoned to a respectable height, but kept it tied at the bottom so her figure wouldn't be lost within all that material. That shouldn't have been a worry for her, though, since her figure wouldn't have been lost if she was wrapped up in a burlap sack.

"My name's Jenny Hatcher," she said. "Didn't Henry tell you I might be looking for you?"

"He mentioned a partner," Clint replied while taking her hand and shaking it. "But he didn't mention how pretty that partner would be."

"Henry's a smart fellow," she said. "He knows better than to dwell on something he can't have."

"Too bad for him," Clint said. "But what about me? Am I allowed to dwell a little bit?"

She grinned, turned on her heels, and started walking briskly into the general store. "We'll have to wait and see about that."

NINETEEN

They were in the store for less than five minutes. Jenny made a straight line down the store's only aisle to a spot in the back next to a little window. She leaned forward to prop her elbows on the window and whistle for the attention of a little old man working in a small room on the other side of that window.

Clint's attention was still firmly fixed upon Jenny. More specifically, he found his eyes settling on the fine contour of her backside as she leaned forward and spoke to the little old man. When she turned around quickly, Jenny didn't seem the least bit surprised to find where Clint's eyes were pointed.

"These are some of the best sandwiches I've ever had," she told him. "I recommend the ham, but you can order what you like."

"You're the expert," Clint replied. "I'll take your word for it, just so long as there's more than just a sandwich."

"It's all you'll need. Trust me."

After that, they were out of the store and walking down the street. Considering how quickly they'd gotten their food, Clint wasn't too hopeful about how good that sandwich would be. At the very least, he had to admit that it would be more than enough to fill his stomach.

Rather than being made with normal-sized bread, each of their sandwiches seemed to have been set up with its own loaf. The things were at least a foot long and big enough for Clint to need both hands to hold his. With the bundle he'd gotten from Dorothy under one arm, Clint brought the sandwich to his mouth and took a bite.

"Good Lord," Clint said through a full mouth. "This is amazing!"

Jenny was already well into her own sandwich, and grinned once she'd swallowed the bite she was working on. "I told you."

The ham was glazed with a thin layer of honey and brown sugar. The bread was still warm from the oven and the mustard was just spicy enough to give every little flavor a spicy kick.

"This is the only time to get them, though," she said. "They're freshly made only twice a day."

"What's the other time?"

"Too early for a ham sandwich."

They were at a corner that was fairly deserted since one of the buildings there was either still being built or was in the process of coming apart. Either way, it left a gap in the storefronts with plenty of good, empty ledges to sit. After taking a load off his feet, Clint waited for Jenny to sit down before he took a break from his sandwich.

"So how long have you been following me?" he asked.

She didn't bat an eye. Instead, she took another bite and savored every bit of it. When she was good and ready, she answered, "Just since you've been in California."

"That's been a few weeks."

"Then maybe a little less. I am the one who gave Henry the news that you were the closest one who could help him regarding this mess."

"You're one of his spies? I'm surprised I never picked you out of a crowd before."

"Oh, no," she said with a laugh. "There are folks looking out for each other everywhere you go. I hate that part of the business. It gives me a chill thinking someone's looking over my shoulder wherever I go."

"Yeah," Clint grunted. "I know just how you feel."

"He admires you, you know."

"Who does? Whiteoak?"

Jenny nodded. "He says you're something like a cross between a saint and a devil because you help out even the lowliest soul with the fury of an animal."

"Sounds like the way he talks, but not quite his words."

"I may have embellished a bit, but that was the high and low of it."

"You've got a good sense for people, Jenny."

She accepted the compliment with a nod. "That's what I do best."

"So where does running a con come into the mix?"

"We've been doing that since we were kids."

"You and Whiteoak?"

"No," she said grimly. "Me and Josh. He was my cousin. He was also the one who showed me a way to make a good living without using a gun or a plow." She caught Clint's eyes wandering along the side of her body, only this time they went to a small holster on her waist. "Well," she added, "I don't use a gun very often."

"Josh was your cousin?"

She nodded in a way that told Clint a lot. There was some sadness there, along with plenty of regret. But more importantly, he knew she wasn't lying.

"I'm sorry," he said.

"Don't be. The one who should be sorry is Teasley. Josh always took more risks than I did. He always knew there was a chance he could get hurt. But that Teasley killed him without even giving him a chance." She tore off a piece of her sandwich and gnawed on it as though she'd had to kill it first. "Shooting him in the back would have been less cowardly."

"Have you found out anything regarding how he died?"

"What does it matter? He's gone and there's no coming back. Anyone in this line of work knows what they're getting in to. We come to terms with that real quick, so we can take the risks normal folks wouldn't."

"You mean folks that aren't crazy?" Clint asked.

"Yeah. Something like that. So far, everything I've heard is that people are getting sick and a few have died. Apart from Josh, the ones who died didn't have anything to do with me, Henry, or even Teasley as far as I know."

"That makes things a bit more difficult."

Clint handed over the bundle that he'd been carrying under his arm.

"What's that?" Jenny asked.

"Your cousin's things."

"Keep them. He didn't carry anything on him that couldn't be replaced."

"He might have picked up something useful before he died."

After a bit of consideration, Jenny nodded and stood up. "Then let's take a look. Only, let's not do it here. If there is something important, I'd rather not do it in front of Teasley's errand boys."

Clint looked up to where Jenny was nodding. Sure enough, there was another familiar face from the Silver Dollar watching them from across the street.

TWENTY

Apart from the obvious advantage of watching Jenny move, Clint found that he was able to learn something from her regarding how to glide through a crowd like a snake through tall grass. Keeping a calm look on her face, she sidestepped at just the right times, pretended to trip over a few nonexistent holes in the road, as well as doing any number of other things to throw off the man trying to keep up with them.

The result was that she was almost impossible to keep in sight from afar. Actually, Clint nearly lost her once or twice and he was directly beside her. They lost their would-be tracker halfway to the hotel where Jenny was staying. Even the hotel itself was easy to miss when walking by on the street.

Since it appeared to be a converted store of some kind, the hotel's lobby was nothing but a small counter and narrow desk. Jenny's was the third out of five rooms in the entire place. Fortunately, the room was comfortable and had a good view of both major streets outside the hotel.

The first thing Jenny did when she got into the room was go to the window and take a look outside. She stood there for quite a while, just surveying the streets through the glass. Finally, she saw enough to satisfy her curiosity and drew the curtains.

"Teasley's too cheap to have hired new men, so we're clear," she reported. "Now, let's take a look at what you got from the doctor."

Clint held the bundle out in one hand and used his other to unwrap it. Just as Jenny had predicted, there wasn't much inside.

"Too bad I didn't catch up to you sooner," she said after sifting through what little was in there. "I could have saved you the trouble of getting this."

"Looks like there might be some personal things in here."

"We don't travel with anything we aren't ready to lose. At least, that's how it was for everyone but Henry. I swear, that dandy would lug around three cedar chests if it was up to him."

"Well, I'll keep this then. Can you tell me where to find Josh's next of kin?"

She looked at him extra carefully as if she was waiting for him to change his mind. When he didn't, she ripped a small piece of paper from something lying on the bed and scribbled on it with a nub of a pencil. "That's his sister's place in Sacramento," she told him. "I don't know if she's still there, but that should at least put you on the right track. You mind if I ask why you're so concerned about a dead trickster you didn't even know?"

"Trickster, huh? You must have spent time with the Indians to pick up that one."

She nodded. "A bit."

"I don't know any of those others that are laying in that doctor's office right now, but I'd like to help them if I could just like I'd like to do what I can for Josh." Clint glanced over at the bundle and shrugged. "Even though I got here a little late."

Jenny didn't glance at the bundle. In fact, she seemed to

have already put it out of her mind completely. Instead, she was more concerned with studying Clint's face and especially his eyes. "Henry mentioned that he knew you. Of course, most of us figured that was just another one of his stories. But when it seemed like he was telling the truth, I figured you were one of those gunfighters with cold eyes and ice in his blood."

Lowering his eyes just a bit, Clint made a subtle move toward her as he felt the heat from her body becoming especially warm. "It sure doesn't feel like ice in my veins right now."

She responded to him instantly, moving closer while reaching out to run her hands along Clint's body. She started at his stomach and slowly eased her palms up to his chest. "No," she whispered. "It sure doesn't."

For a second, both of them stood right where they were and savored the moment. Both of them knew what was coming, but were in no hurry to get there. Both of them had known this was coming since the first time they'd laid eyes on each other.

Clint let his hands drift onto her hips and rested them there as she slowly moved between his palms. Sliding his hands along her smooth curves, Clint found his way to the firm roundness of her buttocks. From there, he pulled her closer until their bodies were pressed against each other.

When their mouths connected, they shared a tentative kiss. As soon as Clint let his tongue drift across Jenny's lips, neither one of them could hold back any longer. Letting out a sigh, Jenny kissed him fiercely while pulling at the buckle of Clint's belt.

TWENTY-ONE

Hands were moving in a flurry and clothes were flying in every direction as Clint and Jenny rushed to get all the way down to bare skin. The moment Clint's hands touched her naked flesh, he felt like a miner who'd finally struck gold.

He'd pulled off her shirt and slipped his hands beneath a thin cotton undershirt that clung to Jenny's body like a second skin. Underneath that shirt, her belly was flat and muscular while her breasts were firm and smooth. The moment he grazed his palm over her nipple, he felt her body respond and heard her let out a passionate moan.

She'd also struck gold, but Jenny had been looking in a slightly different spot. The first thing she did was pull off Clint's pants so she could wrap her hand around his stiff cock. While stroking him, she used her free hand to pull open his shirt and peel it off of him.

Acting on nothing but instinct, Clint got her out of her jeans and onto the bed. To be more precise, he got her onto the edge of the bed, which was just good enough for the time being. She sat down and positioned herself on the corner of the mattress, looking up at him expectantly.

Clint stood as close as he could to her without climbing onto the bed himself. He then reached down, slipped his hands under her thighs, and pulled her a little closer. Jenny's eyes became wide with excitement as she allowed herself to be scooted all the way to the edge.

Clint reached down with one hand between her legs, finding the wet lips of her pussy and stroking them slowly. At first, Jenny was surprised by the sudden intimate contact. But it was the best kind of surprise she could have wanted and it took her breath away almost immediately.

"Oh, my God, that feels good," she purred. When Clint's fingers slipped inside her, she tried to say something else, but only got out a long, shivering moan.

At that moment, Clint felt her take hold of his wrist and guide his hand upward an inch or so. She slowly closed her eyes as she moved his fingers to the sensitive skin of her clitoris. Once he was there, she leaned back and trembled as he rubbed slow circles over her.

Clint watched as Jenny shifted to lean back and support herself with both arms. With just a little coaxing, he got her back a little farther. She had yet to open her eyes again, since Clint was still massaging her. That way, when she felt his rigid penis slide into her, it was enough to make her heart skip a beat.

Jenny's eyes shot open and her mouth formed a silent gasp. Reflexively, she opened her legs for him and thrust her hips forward to accept his first couple of thrusts. After that, she leaned back again and savored the way he moved in and out of her.

Clint let his eyes wander along the front of Jenny's body as he pumped his hips back and forth. Her breasts swayed slightly every time his hips bumped against her and she played with her nipples as if she barely knew she was doing it. Just watching that was more than enough to make Clint even harder.

Taking hold of her hips, he began pulling her to him every time he thrust forward. Eventually, his hands slipped under her so he could massage the inviting curves of her backside as he entered her. Soon, Jenny was lifting her hips again and wriggling inside his hands as if she knew exactly how to send a chill down his spine.

While Jenny's moans became louder, Clint moved forward until he was able to kneel on the edge of the bed. She was lying back and stretching out by now, sifting both hands through her hair so she could fan it out around her head. When she opened her eyes, she watched Clint settle on top of her as if she was in a dream.

Clint took hold of her legs and lifted them up so he could bury himself inside her. When he pushed as deep as he could go, he heard Jenny let out a throaty, satisfied groan.

"Yes, Clint. Right there," she moaned. "That's the spot."

While sliding one hand along the side of Jenny's body, Clint pumped his hips again and again. Although one of her legs slipped out of his grasp, he kept hold of the other one and ran his hand all the way to her inner thigh.

Jenny closed her eyes again and reached out with both hands to run her palms along Clint's bare chest. This time, she was the one to grab hold of his hips. From there, she was able to get him to speed up or slow down the moment it crossed her mind.

Clint had no problem at all with following her direction. After straightening up so he was kneeling between her legs, he reacted to every one of Jenny's touches, which brought her racing toward a powerful climax. When she came, her muscles tightened around Clint and her nipples became rock hard.

Jenny's back arched and her voice got caught in the back of her throat. Finally, she let out her breath and opened her eyes to find Clint looking straight down at her. Before she could say a word, she felt him pump into her again.

Clint drove all the way inside her and when he pulled back, Jenny raised both legs and set them on his shoulders.

Taking hold of her ankles, Clint tightened his grip and started pounding into her even harder. She was so wet between her legs that he glided in and out with ease. The harder he pumped into her, the wetter she became.

Soon, Jenny was tossing her head back and forth and breathing in quick gasps as another orgasm shot through her.

Clint closed his eyes so he could fully savor the way Jenny's warm, wet lips wrapped around him. He pumped into her a few more times as he felt a climax building inside him. As that feeling drew closer, he pounded into her harder until he exploded inside her.

For the next few moments, Clint and Jenny just tried to catch their breaths. Once they did that, it took another few moments until they were able to speak.

Jenny pulled in a deep breath and let it out luxuriously. "Mmm. That was . . . you were . . ."

"Yeah," Clint said with a grin. "My thoughts exactly."

TWENTY-TWO

Henry Whiteoak sat in his room, feeling as if the steak he'd wolfed down was about to work its way back up again. Although he was worried about Clint being gone so long, he didn't have the same urge to get out of the room as he had earlier. In fact, the more he thought about someone getting the best of Clint, the more Whiteoak wanted to gather his things and get out of town.

When he heard the steps approaching his door, he tiptoed over to it and gently placed his ear against the wood. Sure enough, there was someone on the other side. By the sound of it, they were fiddling with their key.

Whiteoak pulled the latch and opened the door. "Where the hell have you . . ." he started to say, but stopped himself short when he saw who was standing in the hall.

The deputy had one hand on his holstered gun and his other hand pressed against the wall. Leaning there, he seemed just as surprised to see the door come open as Whiteoak was at who he found there.

Standing next to the deputy was the man who worked at the hotel's front desk. He was the one fiddling with his keys as he sifted from one to the other on a small ring, looking for the one to fit into that particular lock.

"Looks like I don't need your help after all," the deputy said to the hotel clerk. "You'd best move along so you don't get hurt."

Hearing that was enough to drain all the color from Whiteoak's face. "Hold on just a moment," he said while backing into his room. "There's no need for violence, Seth."

The deputy walked slowly into the room. His gun was still holstered, but his arm was twitching for any excuse to draw it. "And there won't be any so long as you come with me without making a fuss."

"Fuss? Me?"

"Yeah, perish the thought. You're only the man who sliced your way out of town and nearly cut one man's leg off in the process."

"That's got to be an exaggeration!"

"Maybe. Maybe not. Just come with me before I drag you outside by the scruff of your neck."

Only when Whiteoak felt the back of his leg bump against a chair did he stop moving. He shot his hands over his head as if he was being robbed and put on a trembling smile. "Sure thing, Seth. You know I'm not about to make a move against you."

The deputy held his ground and fixed a stern look on Whiteoak. The other man responded by shifting on his feet and then finally raising his right hand a little higher.

"Take it," Whiteoak said as he turned so the gun tucked under his belt was easier to see. "Like I said. No fuss."

After relieving him of his weapon, Seth said, "And the other one. That blade of yours."

Whiteoak wasn't as quick to hand over his straight-edge since that had saved his bacon more than once. Even so, he snapped his wrist and got the straight-edge to fall into the palm of his hand. "You see?" he said as he tossed the straight-edge to Seth. "There's no way I could have cut a man's leg off."

"Yeah, yeah. Is there anything else on you I need to know about?"

"No. I'm completely defenseless."

"Good," the deputy said. Then he pulled Whiteoak's wrists together. In a few quick movements, followed by a few metallic snaps, Whiteoak's wrists were locked into a thick pair of cuffs.

"Now get moving," the deputy said. "You know the way. The sheriff will like to have a word with you."

Whiteoak kept his head down as they left the hotel, unwilling to meet the gaze of the clerk or anyone else for that matter. "If you don't mind me asking, how did you find me?"

"Someone spotted you walking down around Third Avenue. I can tell you weren't there buying clothes."

Whiteoak retraced his steps and realized Third Avenue was in the vicinity of the sewing shop where he'd met up with Jenny. That was the problem with trying to sneak as opposed to blustering your way through. All it took was one set of alert eyes to blow everything to hell.

"I suppose I'm headed for the noose again," Whiteoak croaked.

"That wasn't the sheriff's doing, but you do have to answer for a few things."

A bit of spring entered Whiteoak's steps. "I'm more than willing to stand trial and pay what I owe just like any upstanding citizen."

"Shut up," Seth grunted. "I'm just here to collect you, not to listen to all of your—"

He was cut short by a dull cracking sound that reminded Whiteoak of the flat end of an ax smacking against a log. When he turned to get a look at Seth, he found the deputy staring back at him without a trace of life in his eyes.

The sound came again. This time, however, Whiteoak saw a blur of motion as something was swung from behind Seth's head and connected with the deputy's skull. Blood sprayed through the air and the deputy began to wobble on his legs before slumping to one side and falling to the ground.

Now that Seth had dropped, the way was clear for Whiteoak to see the face of who'd dropped him.

The big man loomed like a mountain and was covered with so much blood that it looked like gruesome paint on his face. In his hand was a small club wrapped in leather and slick with more blood. His ugly, cruel face bore a wide, gap-toothed smile.

"Talk your way out of this, asshole," the big man snarled. He then turned and walked away while casually using his shirttail to wipe some of the blood off his club.

Already, people were taking notice of what was happening as screams started rolling through the air.

TWENTY-THREE

Whiteoak was not a fighting man.

All his life, he'd gotten ahead by talking and thinking his way out of any jam in which he found himself. In Piedmont, however, even a thinking man would be forced to do some fighting if he was going to make it out alive.

Despite the size of the man who'd knocked Seth across the head, the act had been done so quickly and efficiently that it took folks a few seconds to realize something had happened. Once they saw the blood and the fallen deputy, all that was left was Henry Whiteoak rummaging through Seth's pockets.

Ignoring the screams and noises coming from the locals who were swarming in on him from all sides, Whiteoak searched from one of Seth's pockets to the other until he found what he was after. After taking the key to the handcuffs, Whiteoak used it to free his wrists and then gathered up his weapons.

"Sorry about that," he said to the deputy.

But Seth didn't answer back. He wasn't even moving. In fact, the deputy was lying so still that it was fairly obvious he wasn't going to move again.

While stuffing his gun back into place and dropping the

straight-edge into his pocket, Whiteoak ran after the big fellow who'd clubbed Seth over the back of his head. He ran past a few of the locals who'd come by to see what happened, and even shoved aside a few that didn't know enough to step aside. All the while, Whiteoak's eyes were focused in the direction in which the big attacker had gone.

As of yet, there was still no sign of the man.

Whiteoak kept running until the screams and commotion were behind him. He was so focused on trying to pick up the bigger man's trail that he didn't even pay attention to where he was going. Suddenly, Whiteoak found himself in a small lot behind a short row of stores. He still couldn't see the bigger man, but he knew he was close as if he could smell the blood on the attacker's hands.

As Whiteoak rounded the next corner, everything around him seemed to shift into a slower speed. His feet were still tearing into the dirt when his eyes spotted something directly in front of him that wasn't about to move.

The big man had blood smeared across the front of his shirt and seemed bigger and more imposing than a brick wall.

It was all Whiteoak could do to keep from running face-first into that wall before he skidded and fell into a heap.

Surprisingly enough, the big man kept Whiteoak from falling. The downside was that he also kept Whiteoak from escaping.

"You're a quick little bastard," the big man said. "I'll give you that much. You think you can run fast enough to get away from the sheriff once he sees his deputy laying in the street?"

Whiteoak's first impulse was to take a swing at the big man. His knuckles bounced uselessly off the man's chest, but that allowed him to pluck the pistol from where it had been wedged under his belt. The moment he felt that heavy iron in his hand, Whiteoak swung it at the big man like a mallet.

Although this was also a glancing blow, the gun's barrel carried a little more of an impact. It forced the big man's fist open just long enough for Whiteoak to slip out and take a few quick steps back.

"Why did you kill that man?" Whiteoak asked in between wheezing breaths.

The big man shrugged as if he was engaging in a leisurely conversation. "Business," was all he said before leaning forward and taking a swing at Whiteoak's face.

That fist was coming at him so quickly that Whiteoak barely had time to notice the bloody club gripped in the middle of it. He threw himself back, losing his balance in the process, and tried desperately to regain his footing. The club cut through the air just over his head with such ferocity that he knew he wouldn't have survived if it had landed. Whiteoak didn't have much of a chance to savor his small victory, since another swing was already headed straight for him.

The big man snarled as he sent his club at its target one more time. This time it was with a backhanded strike that lacked some of the power of the one before it. The swing didn't land either, due to the fact that Whiteoak was still scrambling back.

Instead of simply fighting to survive, Whiteoak managed to keep enough of his wits about him to lift his gun and take a shot. The pistol barked once and sent a bullet into the big man's shoulder. That chunk of lead might as well have been lodged in a thick mass of cured beef, however, since it didn't seem to affect the man who'd gotten shot.

The big man winced a bit and paused just long enough to toss his club from the hand on his wounded arm into his other one. "The doc was right about you. I never would'a believed you'd be this hard to kill."

"What business is this concerning?" Whiteoak asked while trying to keep his gun hand from trembling. "What were you talking about?"

But the big man didn't even seem to hear the questions coming at him. In fact, he didn't even seem to care much about the gun being pointed at him. Instead, his free hand snapped out to slap aside Whiteoak's gun as that bloody club whipped through the air toward Whiteoak's head.

As Whiteoak reflexively closed his eyes, he twisted to one side as though he meant to curl up in a ball and rock himself to sleep. Whether the move was quick enough or unexpected enough didn't much matter. All that did matter was that it was enough to get him out of the way of yet another powerful swing.

The club sliced downward to graze a crate that had been stacked nearby. The impact knocked the side off the crate with ease and the sound of splintering wood mingled with the snarl coming from the big man's throat.

As Whiteoak looked up, he saw the ferocity in the big man's eyes. That man's single purpose was to cave in Whiteoak's skull and any fool could tell that Whiteoak couldn't dodge him forever.

TWENTY-FOUR

The big man's arm swung down toward Whiteoak's forehead like an ax finding its way to an exposed neck. Whiteoak's finger tightened around his trigger and the gun bucked against his palm, but even that wasn't enough to divert the club.

Another shot cracked through the air, leaving Whiteoak to wonder what it would take to put the big man down. Then, just as he closed his eyes and was bracing for the impact of that club against his temple, Whiteoak started to feel dizzy.

The club had yet to fall and a few seconds had already ticked by. It wasn't a lot of time, but it should have been more than enough for the big man to finish him off.

Slowly, reluctantly, Whiteoak tried to peel open his eyes.

"What the hell's going on here, Henry?" a vaguely familiar voice asked. "Are you all right?"

Although he'd been trying to do so, Whiteoak hadn't yet managed to get his eyes open. When he heard that voice, however, his eyelids couldn't lift quickly enough.

"Is that you, Clint?"

"Yeah, Henry," Clint said. "It's me. I heard shooting around here."

"Yeah," Whiteoak sputtered as he tried to pull himself together. "I fired off a shot or two . . . I think."

"Well, did it have anything to do with that deputy that was killed?" When he didn't see Whiteoak trying to give an answer, Clint took hold of the man's shoulder and gave him a few quick shakes. "Henry, you'd better get your head together because there's a whole lot that needs to be explained here."

Whiteoak shook his head and then shook free of Clint's grasp. Looking down at the gun in his hand brought everything flooding right back into Whiteoak's head whether he wanted it there or not. "I was being brought in by Seth."

"That's the deputy?" Clint asked while looking over his shoulder.

"Yeah. I try to find out about as many of the lawmen as I can after I get into a town before I—"

"You can cut through all that and tell me what happened."

"Right, right," Whiteoak said. "I was brought into custody and we were ambushed."

"Who ambushed you?"

"It was a big fellow. Real ugly, as well."

Clint's brow furrowed and he rattled off a quick description of the man who'd attacked him. Even before he was done with his description, Clint could see the look of recognition on Whiteoak's face.

"Yes!" Whiteoak said. "That's the man! That's him!"

"Well, he's certainly big enough to have caved in that poor deputy's skull. I had a hard time believing it when I heard folks saying it was you."

"What?" Whiteoak yelped. "Who said that?"

"Some of the folks gathering around the deputy's body," Clint explained. "I came running when I heard the law shouting that one of their own was killed. Some of the folks already there were talking quite a bit."

"Damn. That was fast. I've only just now started to catch my breath, and already there's scuttlebutt going around about what happened."

"People around here have been on edge lately, especially now that word's been getting out that more folks have taken ill."

"Good Lord," Whiteoak said.

"Yeah, but we can't worry about that right now. Where's the man who attacked you?"

"I don't know."

"Then who were you shooting at?" Clint demanded. "You've got to remember something, otherwise he'll get away!"

"That way," Whiteoak said as his hand snapped up to point away from him.

Clint looked in that direction and saw nothing but the narrow mouth of an alleyway. "Are you sure about that?"

"No, but that's the only way he could have gone. Otherwise, you would have run into him yourself."

"Good point. Come along with me and get that gun of yours ready."

Whiteoak's eyes became wide as saucers as he squeaked, "What? You want me to go with you?"

"Would you rather stay here and deal with another lynch mob?"

Almost immediately, Whiteoak started nodding. "I'll show you the way."

As Clint walked down the alley, he searched for any trace of the big man. Meanwhile, his mind went over his last fight with that same man, and he recalled just how fast the man had moved. Considering the time that had already passed, Clint knew his chances of catching up to him were very slim indeed if the big man was trying to get away.

"What else have you been able to come up with, Henry?" Clint asked.

"In what regard?"

"In regard to the reason we came here! I've seen the folks that are sick and it's only getting worse. You're the one who knows about all this kind of thing and you wanted me to get you into town to deal with it, so what can you do?"

Whiteoak was twisting and turning as he moved in an effort to look in every direction at once. "I was hoping to get a sample of something that was poisoned," he said while flinching at yet another shadow. "So far, all I've had was some cold steak."

"And you're still certain that Teasley is the man we should look at?"

"Almost definitely."

"Almost might not quite cut it," Clint warned.

"That's the best I can do. Anything more, and I would just be trying to make you feel better."

"I doubt that would make me feel any better, but I see what you're saying." Clint stopped as the alley opened into one of the larger streets in town. Looking over his shoulder only confirmed that they'd passed a long stretch of solid walls. "He's gone."

Even though he hadn't wanted to hear that, Whiteoak knew those words would be coming. When he heard the sound of angry voices drawing closer, he felt his blood race through his veins. "What should we do now?"

"I met up with your partner," Clint said. "She's staying at a hotel not far from here. Go meet up with her and see if you can come up with a way to get close enough to Teasley so you might be able to get a bottle of whatever it is he serves to customers he doesn't like."

"How can we do that?"

"You're a swindler and a con man," Clint said dryly. "I'm sure the two of you can come up with something. Just remember to keep your face hidden as best you can. I think I might be able to steer this mess back in the proper direction."

Glancing toward the approaching voices, Whiteoak asked, "You mean them?"

"They're angry, but they're still confused. That gives us a little breathing room. Just go and try to look in on Teasley and I'll try to keep the heat off of you."

Whiteoak nodded. "That should help. What are you going to do?"

"Leave that to me," Clint said sternly. "And if you manage to get what you need, don't wait around to hear from me. I'll try to stay in touch, but we can't waste any more time. This thing isn't going to get better on its own, so we need to do whatever it takes to set it right. You hear me, Henry? Anything."

Letting out a breath, Whiteoak nodded grimly. "If it comes to that, I'll walk right up to the sheriff and hand him the antidote. Lynch mob be damned."

Clint didn't spot the first hint of deception in Whiteoak's eyes. Now, more than ever, he remembered why he'd agreed to help the man in the first place. "All right then. Good luck."

"We're both going to need it."

TWENTY-FIVE

No matter how confident he'd sounded a few seconds ago, Clint wasn't able to feel so confident through and through. The ugly truth was that people were dead, others were dying, and things hadn't been getting any better since he'd arrived.

Clint kept his gun in hand as he worked his way back through the alley. Once he got to the spot where he'd found Whiteoak, Clint hunkered down and started taking a close look around. There wasn't much to see, so he did his best to study the ground where the fight had taken place. It wasn't much, but he was more than willing to grasp at a few straws right about then.

Thanks to the fight and the short-lived chase that had followed, Clint saw nothing on the ground apart from a whole mess of overlapping tracks and scuffs in the dirt. His eyes darted frantically back and forth as a few of the braver locals worked up the courage to investigate the previous gunshots for themselves.

Clint found his eyes drifting in a particular pattern, even though he didn't know exactly why they were going that way. Once he took a moment to focus on the ground rather than the voices that were getting closer and closer, he saw what it was that had caught his attention.

Instead of looking at the shapes in the dirt, he shifted his focus on something else. More specifically, there was a color smeared on the ground that didn't seem to belong. Clint reached down to touch one of the larger smears, which were lying amid the useless mess of overlapping tracks.

The color that he'd spotted reminded him of dried blood or even rust. Once his fingers touched the smear, he felt a texture that told him the color was neither of those things. It was too thick to be flakes of rust and too smooth to be blood.

People were starting to walk up to him, spouting off everything from threats to accusations, but Clint ignored them all. Instead, he used his other hand to scrape into the ground before finally shoving his fingers deep into the dirt. When he pulled that hand out, he looked at it with a growing smile.

"Hey!" came a sharp voice that cut through all the others. "Just what are you doing there?"

Clint turned around to see who was talking, but found himself staring right down the barrel of a pistol. Getting to his feet, he took a quick measure of the man behind that gun.

"You're the sheriff?" Clint asked, noting the badge pinned to the man's chest.

"That's right. Would that make you the man who killed my deputy?"

"No, sir."

One of the locals who'd tagged along with the sheriff started to run forward, but was quickly wrangled away by another deputy. "It was him!" the local shouted.

"The hell it was!" another person chimed in. "Not even close!"

The sheriff addressed his deputy without taking his eyes

away from Clint. "Clear these loudmouths out of here! Go around to the ones that have something helpful to say and take their statements."

With a quick nod, the deputy followed through on the orders he'd been given. In no time at all, the small lot was fairly quiet again.

"Are you Clint Adams?" the sheriff asked.

"I am."

"I'm Sheriff Morton. Teasley's been talking about you, but I thought he was full of it. One time he said he had Wild Bill in his place, but that was a few days after he'd been killed."

"I'd be happy to talk to you, Sheriff, but it would ease my nerves if you lowered that gun."

"Talk first, Adams. I like my chances better the way things are."

Clint made sure to keep his movements short, so as not to provoke the sheriff. Despite the gun in the lawman's hand, there was something about him that told Clint he wasn't out of chances just yet. "I saw the man who hit your deputy."

"Killed my deputy," Sheriff Morton corrected.

Clint nodded. "He attacked me not too long ago. He's big and strong as an ox, but quick as a jackrabbit. Tough too. He's been wounded at least twice, but that doesn't seem to slow him down."

"Awfully convenient to have a man like that around. Too bad he's nowhere to be seen."

"If I'd just bushwhacked a deputy, I'd make myself scarce as well."

"I see your point, Adams. Keep talking."

The gun in Morton's hand lowered just a bit, but remained pointed at Clint.

"There's some handcuffs back there," Clint said, while nodding in the direction where the deputy's body had been left. "The tracks lead back here, where there's obviously been a struggle. I heard someone mention an escaped prisoner."

Morton nodded. "By the looks of it, I'd say he's the one I'm after."

"That is, unless he only got away after your deputy was attacked."

"A prisoner has plenty of reason to escape. Especially this one."

"But would the prisoner you're thinking of be able to overpower a lawman and cave in the back of his head?" Clint asked. Even though his words got no reaction from the sheriff, Clint could see they were at least getting through to him.

A couple of locals stormed toward the lot, shouting what they'd seen along with what they thought they'd seen every step of the way. The sheriff didn't bat an eye as those locals were corralled and dragged away from him and Clint.

"What did you see here, Adams?" Morton asked once things had died down again.

"I got here just as that that big fellow was getting away. I just caught a glimpse of him before he fired a shot at me and slipped out of my sight." Although he had Morton pegged as a good man, Clint didn't have enough time to be perfectly honest with the man. Instead, he would take Whiteoak at his word and see what he could build from there.

"When I came back here to get a look for myself, I found this," Clint said as he held out the hand he'd been using to feel the substance he'd found just beneath the tracks.

"What's that supposed to be?" Morton asked.

"It's clay. I noticed that the ground in this area doesn't have much of this stuff around."

The sheriff leaned in to get a better look at Clint's fingers. He didn't have to look too closely before he shook his head and leaned back again. "Not around here maybe, but I know where you could find plenty of that stuff."

"Where's that?"

"The creek just west of here. The banks are that very color in a few spots."

"Is that the only place where this stuff can be found?"

"Far as I know, and I've lived here a good portion of my life."

"Take a look for yourself," Clint said while stepping aside so Morton could do just that. "Someone tracked that clay into this lot. Since it's not all over the place, I'd say it was only one of the men that have been through here most recently."

Glancing at the spot where Clint had been searching, Morton moved over there to get a look for himself. He brushed aside some of the looser dirt with the toe of his boot and then nodded confidently. "Any local knows that stuff when they see it and I'm looking at it right now."

"Does anyone live down by the creek that might have a hand in this?"

The sheriff let out a sigh, but he also holstered his gun. "That creek runs through plenty of towns other than this one. It leads all the way to the Pacific, to be exact. Lord only knows how many folks track that shit on the bottom of their boots. It's bad enough that most local stores will fine you if you don't wipe your feet before stepping into their places. Give me a look at your boots."

Adams lifted one boot and then the other so the lawman could get a look at their soles. There wasn't a trace of clay to be seen. Just then, one of the deputies wandered into the lot.

"Seth was going after that Whiteoak fella," the deputy said. "Had him in shackles and was dragging him back when someone jumped him."

"You sure about that?"

"Yes, sir, Sheriff. Old Man Peters saw it from his window and a few folks back him up. As for Seth going after Whiteoak, James verifies that part of it personally."

"Looks like your story holds up, Adams, and so do your boots. But I shouldn't have to tell you how bad it'll look if you decide to clear out of town before all of this gets straightened out."

"Don't worry about that," Clint assured him. "I'm real interested to see how this pans out."

TWENTY-SIX

Jenny was sitting on her bed when she heard something scratching at her window. Her first impulse was to grab for the gun she kept hidden under her belt. Before she had a chance to draw, however, her window was already coming open. When it opened all the way, she made sure to have her gun in her hand and ready to fire.

"Oh, my God," she said when she saw someone practically jump through the open window. "Is that you, Henry?"

Whiteoak made a less than graceful entrance and landed in a heap beneath the window. Even though he twisted his ankle on the way in, he gathered himself up quickly and pressed his back to the wall. "Is anyone following me?" he asked in a rush.

Accustomed to this sort of thing, Jenny moved to the window and took a careful look outside. When she was done, she closed the window, made sure it was locked, and then drew the curtains. "There's a lot of people in the street, but they don't seem to be looking this way. What the hell happened to you?"

Whiteoak gave her a quick account of what had happened and wrapped it up with: "Clint bought me some time and I came here as quickly as I could."

"You just left Clint there?"

"I didn't have much of a choice. Besides, I was the one in danger. Whoever that monster was, he was long gone."

"Sounds like he did a real good job of setting you up before he left."

Still breathing in gasps, Whiteoak slowed himself down and then felt his thoughts falling into place. "He sure did. Good Lord. Who would want to do something like this?"

Jenny winced, but allowed her shoulders to give a wary shrug.

"All right," Whiteoak conceded. "But who on that list is actually responsible for it this time?"

"I don't know, but I do think that Josh might have known a bit more than we might have originally guessed."

"Josh?"

She nodded and made her way back to the edge of the bed where she'd been sitting. "Clint got his things from the doctor's office and gave them to me since I'm Josh's cousin and all."

"I guess there's no way for him to know how much you and Josh fought."

"What's that supposed to mean?"

Whiteoak blinked a few times as if he'd been smacked on the nose. "Just that he wouldn't have given you Josh's things if he knew you'd probably just toss them out with the trash."

Even though she was still angry, Jenny couldn't deny the truth in what Whiteoak was saying. Nobody was that good an actor. "You're right," she finally sighed. "But I have been going through these things. You know, despite everything he did, all the times he cheated me and all the bullshit he put me through, I still am going to miss him."

"Yeah. Just like you'd miss a screeching cat that never shut up or gave you a moment's peace."

"Yes," she said. "Something like that." Suddenly, Jenny shook herself out of her thoughts and pushed aside most of the things that had been in that bundle. "Most of this stuff is just whatever was in his pockets when he fell sick. All of it except for this."

Jenny held something in her hand and extended her arm toward Whiteoak. Opening three of her four fingers allowed something to fall from her palm and dangle between her thumb and forefinger.

Whiteoak squinted and leaned forward to get a better look. "What is that? A necklace?"

"Try a locket," Jenny corrected. "And it didn't belong to Josh."

"Are you sure?"

"Definitely. I went through his things more than enough times to have stumbled upon this if it was ever there." When she caught Whiteoak's questioning glare, she added, "Maybe Josh wasn't the only one who was an ass over the years. Anyway, this didn't belong to him and it didn't belong to me. Is it yours?"

Whiteoak shook his head. "Never seen it before in my life."

"Then that's what makes it interesting," she said with a victorious smile. "Just have a look for yourself."

Saying that, Jenny carefully cradled the locket in the palm of one hand while easing it open. She took a pace that was almost maddeningly slow. Although the locket was definitely pretty, it didn't look especially rare or nearly fragile enough to warrant such care. But Jenny went through those deliberate motions anyway, and just as Whiteoak was about to hurry her along, she got it open.

"Don't get too close," she warned in a whisper. "I already spilled some of this when I found it the first time."

Inside the locket was a corner of an old picture wedged into the frame after having been torn out. The rest of the space inside the locket was covered with a gray, almost silvery powder that resembled metal filings.

"What is that?" Whiteoak asked.

"I don't know. I was hoping you'd be able to tell me. Smell it."

At first, Whiteoak looked at her as though she was crazy. Then, he took a hesitant sniff. Pausing, he cocked his head slightly and replaced his skeptical expression with one of sudden recognition. "I know that smell."

Jenny grinned and said, "So do I. It's one of the powders you keep in those jars in your wagon. I recognized the smell the moment I opened that locket! What is it?"

"It's a strong chemical that shouldn't be ingested. You didn't taste it or sniff too much of it, did you?"

"No. I just spilled some on the bed. Is this part of some kind of poison?"

"No," Whiteoak said as he dabbed his finger into the powder, "but it might be part of a cure."

TWENTY-SEVEN

No matter how discouraged the sheriff had seemed about narrowing down Clint's search based on that one clue, Eclipse was anxious for a run, so Clint saddled him up. The sun was almost completely down by the time he rode out of Piedmont, which cast a glorious reflection upon the waters of the neighboring creek.

On the outskirts of town, there was a small mill driven by the same waters that flowed straight into Piedmont. The creek was as clear as crystal, which explained why it was a major source of drinking water for the locals. The brilliant reflections and glittering displays playing across the top of the water made it a real easy path to follow. In fact, Clint had to keep himself from simply enjoying his ride.

It was nice to be away from town and all the chaos inside it. It was nice just to put some distance between himself and Whiteoak. Just listening to the flow of the water and hearing the birds gathering around to drink was enough to put Clint's mind at ease.

In the next couple of seconds, however, he forced himself out of that train of thought and got his mind back to the task at hand. That creek might have flowed through more than one town before reaching the Pacific, but it didn't hurt for him to go and have a look for himself.

Once the sun was down and the last traces of light were gone from the sky, Clint was able to get a real good look at the surrounding land. A subtle glow in the distance caught his eye and when he looked at it through his spyglass, he caught sight of what had to be a neighboring town.

He didn't know the name of the place right offhand, but the glow of lanterns in several windows along with the movement of another set of locals was enough to make Clint nod and lower the spyglass. If it came down to it, he might have to take the short ride into that other town and start looking for the man he was after.

The only drawback to that plan was the simple fact that he didn't know exactly who he was after just yet. That thought sank to the bottom of his stomach and sat there like a lump of coal.

Even though there wasn't much light to see by, there was a three-quarter moon in the sky, which was more than enough to cast a pale glow onto the creek. The slowly moving water spread that light around just far enough for Clint to get a fairly good look at the banks of the creek. Since the banks in this area were mostly rocks and bushes, he snapped Eclipse's reins and moved along.

After a mile or so, the bushes thinned out and the rocks gave way to a smoother surface. Allowing Eclipse to stop for a moment and taste some of that water for himself, Clint swung down from the saddle and walked up to the edge of the creek.

He stooped down and swiped his hand along the ground. Sure enough, his fingers slid across a slick, muddy surface, which left a stain on his skin resembling rust or blood. It looked darker in the moonlight, but he knew well enough that he'd found a large patch of the clay he'd been looking for.

Moving his gaze along the creek, Clint saw spots very much like the one he'd found all along the waterline. After washing off his hand, Clint took a drink from the water and let the cool liquid trickle down his throat.

"All right, boy," he said to the Darley Arabian. "We've got a long walk ahead of us, so let's get moving."

It took a bit of convincing to get Eclipse away from the water's edge, but the stallion eventually followed Clint's lead.

As he walked, Clint turned his thoughts away from who specifically he was looking for and more toward what sort of person he was after. Using what he already knew, he pieced together that the person must have a good knowledge of chemicals or at least have connections to someone else who did.

The person must have a gripe against Piedmont big enough to justify murder in his own mind.

The person must have the ferocity to follow through on those plans, or must be able to hire someone who does.

What gave Clint some hope was the notion that the person he was after had to be in or around Piedmont itself.

If another town was in the grip of an epidemic, news would have gotten to Piedmont by now. While not good for Piedmont, it at least seemed to be the focal point, and that meant whoever was doing this would need to be, or want to be, close enough to see what they were doing.

These pieces fit perfectly into place as Clint walked along the edge of the creek. He knew he was on to something when he saw the lone wagon sitting on the other side of the water, nestled right in a patch of thick, dark red clay.

TWENTY-EIGHT

The wagon by itself wasn't nearly enough to raise Clint's suspicions. On any night, he might have ridden right past it without a second thought. But this wasn't any night and Clint was looking for something very much like this wagon.

First of all, it was close to town and in a perfect spot to coat a man's boots with clay.

Second, there was a guard walking around the wagon as if on patrol.

And third, the wagon reminded Clint of another wagon he'd seen a few years ago. That wagon had belonged to Henry Whiteoak, who most definitely had a good amount of knowledge regarding chemicals, tonics, and drugs of all shapes and sizes.

As Clint tied Eclipse to a tree that was far enough away from the creek to keep the stallion out of sight, he wasn't suspecting Whiteoak of any wrongdoing. But someone in Whiteoak's trade could most definitely be the culprit. In fact, that possibility seemed so likely that Clint was amazed he hadn't considered it before.

Rather than kick himself for anything like that, Clint kept his head down and his eyes open as he approached the wagon from another side just in case he'd been spotted before. His left hand was stretched in front of him to feel for branches or anything else that might trip him up. His right hand remained on top of his modified Colt.

Clint moved slowly enough that his footsteps blended almost completely into the sound of the water and breeze. Although the guard was fairly light on his feet as well, he wasn't paying nearly as much attention to his surroundings. At least that told Clint that he hadn't been spotted.

When he got to a spot where there was a cluster of bushes, Clint hunkered down and kept perfectly still. He waited there for a few minutes so he could watch the guard walk slowly around the wagon. Every so often, someone would move inside the wagon itself, but there didn't seem to be more than that single guard on patrol.

Now that he had the guard's pattern in mind, Clint started creeping closer and closer to the creek. The water appeared to be fairly shallow, but Clint didn't have any way to be sure. At least, there was no way that would be quick enough that he wouldn't be spotted.

Pulling in a breath, Clint waited for the guard to turn his back to the water before approaching the bed of clay. Clint had his eye on a good-sized rock, which he pulled from the clay and tossed in a high arc. After a few seconds, the rock came down and landed with a loud thump.

Without making a sound, the guard stopped in his tracks and looked toward the noise that he'd just heard. To his credit, the fellow did look in every other direction before hurrying off toward the spot where that rock had landed. Thankfully, however, the guard moved in that direction with his gun held at the ready.

Seeing how the guard reacted gave Clint a bit more information. Mainly, it let him know that there was something important he was guarding. It also told him that the gunman was ready to hurt someone who happened to wander too close to that wagon.

Keeping that in mind, Clint started moving in a bit closer to the very spot where he knew he wasn't wanted.

His first few steps into the creek did nothing but get his boots wet. The creek was about ten or twelve feet across, so it was going to take several more steps for him to reach the other side. Just as that was going through his mind, Clint felt his heel slide off a submerged rock and his leg plunge into a deep section of the creek.

Clint fought back the surprised yelp, which came reflexively to his throat. His arms reached out to brace his fall, but he stopped those as well before they made a splash that would be loud enough to wake the dead. All of that may have been quiet, but it resulted in him dropping down far enough for his mouth to be filled with ice-cold creek water.

Every muscle in Clint's body was bracing for the water to flow over his head.

Panic swept through him for a moment as he planned several steps ahead as to how he would deal with the guard after avoiding drowning.

Then, he suddenly realized that he wasn't actually going to have to worry about that.

The water was just over Clint's nose, but it wasn't over his head. His boots had hit bottom, leaving the top part of his face and his hat high and dry. All Clint had to do was stand on his tiptoes so he could pull in a breath through his nostrils.

His eyes were still wide-open with the shock of his sudden fall when Clint saw the guard come rushing back to the edge of the creek. As much as Clint had tried to stay quiet, there really wasn't much of a way for him to slip and fall like an idiot while also maintaining his silent approach.

Moonlight shone off the barrel of the guard's gun and his footsteps slammed against the hard-packed clay as he came around the wagon and into Clint's sight. Because of the cold water and the excitement rushing through Clint's body, the guard seemed to be moving through a sea of molasses.

Even though Clint knew his reflexes were just buying him a bit of time, he also knew he couldn't afford to waste a fraction of a second. With the guard rushing toward him and his own Colt thoroughly submerged, Clint did the only thing he could do by sucking in a quick breath and bending at the knees.

As the water closed around Clint's head like a cold hand, a churning sound filled his ears. Every scrape of his boots against the bottom became a loud roar and every gurgle in the back of his throat seemed to echo in every direction.

Clint's muscles tensed at the bracing cold, making it hard to move and frighteningly easy to sink even lower. When he looked up, the moon wavered like a glowing lily pad floating over his head. Dark shapes swirled in his vision, one of which was the guard, who was already at the edge of the creek and looking in over the barrel of his shotgun.

TWENTY-NINE

The guard could still hear those sounds echoing through his ears. Whether something had fallen or someone had taken awfully big steps, the guard knew that there'd been some sort of movement nearby. As he approached the creek, he tightened his grip on his shotgun and tensed his finger on the trigger.

His eyes narrowed as he saw proof that he wasn't chasing shadows or some energetic varmint. It was right there in the creek, plain as day. The guard lined up his shotgun on his target, but waited before pulling the trigger. He only had two shots, so he knew better than to waste a single one of them.

Clint crouched at the bottom of that creek as the guard loomed directly over him. If the water wasn't so cold, he might have felt his fingers wrap around his modified Colt. Even if the powder was wet, he could at least club the guard with the iron barrel. Then again, considering that he was completely submerged, Clint doubted he could get enough power in his swing to do much damage.

And there was always the more pressing concern that the guard could pull his own trigger before Clint could do

much of anything about it. Suddenly, a phrase regarding
fish in a barrel sprang into Clint's mind.

It had only been a second or two since Clint had
dropped, but he was already feeling his lungs start to itch.
That guard wouldn't even have to use his shotgun as long
as he kept Clint under long enough to drown. With that in
mind, Clint prepared to lunge out of the water and take his
chances against that shotgun.

Hopefully, surprise would be on his side. At the very
least, Clint knew he'd rather die fighting than cowering at
the bottom of some creek.

And then, just as he was about to make his final move,
Clint saw something that made him hold back and stay
perfectly still.

At least . . . for another couple of seconds.

After studying the water some more, the guard took a look
around at the surrounding bank. He didn't see anything
else out there, so he shifted his eyes back to what he'd
spotted in the creek itself. Keeping his shotgun in one
hand, he reached out with his other to grab the hat floating
on the water.

Picking up the hat, the guard turned it over and looked
inside as if there might actually be something in there.
When he saw nothing but a band and some more water, he
stood up and started to walk away.

Before taking another step, the guard turned to look
back at the creek. He glanced up and down the flat strip of
water, and then took yet another glance at the surrounding
land. Suddenly, the guard felt more than a little stupid.

"Probably some drunk lost it," the guard muttered.

From there, he walked toward the wagon, tossed the hat
against a wheel, and continued walking until he fell right
back into the ruts he'd already worn into the ground.

●   ●   ●

Clint fought the impulse to rush up to the top of the water and fill his lungs with air. Instead, he slowly straightened his legs, pushed up from the bottom, arched his back, and then lifted his chin until his face broke the surface of the creek.

The night air against his wet skin felt even colder than it had underwater, but the breath he took was a better feeling than anything else in recent memory. He didn't realize how cloudy his head had gotten until all of that was chased away by another couple of deep inhales.

When he started to walk forward, Clint quickly knocked his knee against a jagged rock wall. After a bit of turning and feeling with both hands, Clint realized he was standing in a deep pit in the bottom of the creek that wasn't much bigger around than his own arm span.

When he crawled out of that pit in the middle of the creek, Clint realized that the hole had saved his life or the life of that guard. At the very least, it had kept him from being discovered while crossing a creek that was mostly only a foot or two deep.

Suddenly, he had to fight to keep back the urge to laugh at the same predicament he'd thought was going to kill him only moments ago.

THIRTY

After sloshing out of the water, Clint fished out the driest bullets he could find from his gun belt and replaced the soaked ones in the cylinder. Hopefully, he wouldn't have to test those rounds when his life was hanging in the balance. Deciding to leave his hat where it was lying, Clint eased up to the side of the wagon and pressed his ear against it.

There wasn't much to hear apart from a few occasional steps and the clinking of glass. The wagon was large enough for one or two people to stand up inside, although they would be very cramped. By the sound of it, Clint figured there was only one in there at the moment. If there were any more, he would have heard them bumping against each other.

Whoever was in there now didn't speak and didn't stay still for more than a few seconds at a time. Finally, Clint leaned forward and tried to figure out a way to see inside. Listening wouldn't do him any more good since he'd already heard all he could just standing in the vicinity of the wagon.

Clint was just about to move toward one of the small windows on the side of the wagon when he heard the guard's footsteps drawing closer. Doing his best to time his movements to the guard's own sounds, Clint dropped down and got under the wagon.

After rolling onto his stomach, he looked out toward the back of the wagon and saw the guard's boots step up and come to a stop. Like clockwork, the guard paused for a few seconds, took a deep breath, and got moving again. By the time he was a few steps away from the wagon, Clint was already crawling out from underneath it.

Clint had an idea, and started moving quickly to put it into motion. Although the guard seemed bored and predictable enough for the moment, Clint wasn't about to bet on him staying that way forever. Clint ran around the wagon, picked up his hat, and then moved around to the back.

Just as he'd figured, there was a narrow door at the rear of the wagon with a small amount of light trickling out from the inside. Clint kept still for a little while as he counted under his breath. Once he figured he'd waited long enough, he tossed the hat a few yards out, knocked loudly on the wagon's door, and then headed for the shadows a few yards away.

The door came open halfway as the light from inside was blocked. Soon, the door swung open all the way and a solidly built man with thick, dark gray hair stuck his head out. His eyes were close-set and the bottom half of his face was covered with a well-trimmed, finely sculpted goatee.

The man with the goatee looked around for a while before he squinted and finally spotted the hat. He took another look, but his face had a decidedly more confused expression on it. Hesitantly, the man stepped out of the wagon and started looking in all directions.

Clint held his ground, knowing well enough that he was far enough away from the reflections cast off the water to be in total darkness. In fact, the shadow he'd chosen wrapped around him like a thick, black coat. Even though Clint could barely see his own hand in front of him, he couldn't help but get anxious when the man with the goatee looked directly at him.

For a few seconds, the man kept his gaze pointed at Clint. Then, he walked over to the hat lying on the ground and picked it up. Still confused, the man examined the hat until the guard came walking back to the wagon.

"What's this?" the man asked.

The guard shrugged and replied, "Found it floating in the creek, Mr. Colfield."

Colfield nodded and asked, "Did you knock on my door?"

After thinking about it, the guard shook his head. "Nope."

"Did you bump against it?"

"No, sir. You said you didn't want to be disturbed."

Letting out a heavy sigh, Colfield tossed Clint's hat toward the river and took a few more steps away from the wagon. "Feels like I haven't set foot from there for months. The fresh air sure feels nice."

"I wouldn't mind going into town," the guard replied. "I can think of a few other things that would feel nice right about now."

Although Colfield didn't share the guard's leering grin, he did nod warily. "We'll be going into town soon enough, but it won't be for any leisure activities. In fact, you might have a difficult time finding anyone in that town healthy enough to indulge in such things for quite a while."

"How much longer will you be working, Mr. Colfield?"

"I can't say for certain, but it shouldn't be much longer. Have you heard any news from Boris?"

The guard nodded. "He's been real busy. He met up with that Whiteoak fella."

"And?"

"And he set him up real good, just like you asked. I told some deputy Whiteoak was in town and he went straightaway to round him up. Boris caught him walking out of the hotel, as easy as pie. Whiteoak wriggled away, but everyone in town still thinks it was him who killed that deputy."

"You know that for certain?"

Nodding, the guard said, "I spread the word myself. Just like starting a fire. After what Whiteoak pulled last time he was there, folks don't have any problem believing the worst about him."

"For a scoundrel like Whiteoak, that's not very much of a stretch of the imagination. You said he got away. What happened?"

"Wasn't nothing, Mr. Colfield. Him and his hired gun chased after Boris, but they didn't make it far."

"Hired gun?"

The smug grin on the guard's face faded a bit. "Man by the name of Adams. Boris met up with him too. He says he didn't have any trouble with him, but he could be a problem. I don't think he's the type to be taken too lightly."

"So Whiteoak didn't come back unprepared?" Colfield mused. "I guess I shouldn't be too surprised. He doesn't have the nerve to handle his business on his own. I just wish I could be there to see his face as all this hell rains down on him."

"What about Adams? Boris wanted to know what to do if he runs into him again."

"Kill him," Colfield said after taking a moment to think. "Tell Boris to make it public and messy. Ideally, Whiteoak should be there to see it. But if the opportunity presents itself, Boris should do whatever is necessary. I've got work to do and when I'm done, that hired gun will be only one of many bodies laying in the streets of that town."

THIRTY-ONE

Clint only heard the first few sentences of the conversation between Colfield and the man guarding the wagon. That was due to the fact that he was too busy sneaking from shadow to shadow so he could get close enough to that wagon to take a look inside.

As he moved as quickly and quietly as possible, Clint still kept his ears open in an effort to try and catch some of what was being said. He caught a few bits here and there, but his main concern was still in getting to that wagon without being seen. Clint had hoped to buy a few seconds with his little trick, but the old "knock and run" game was working even better than he'd hoped.

Not wanting to waste a moment of the time he'd bought himself, Clint worked his way up to the wagon and pressed his back against the wooden wheel. By this time, Colfield and the guard were involved with their own discussion while Colfield kept his back to the wagon.

Colfield seemed more than happy to keep the wagon out of the guard's sight for a few minutes, and it was easier on the guard's eyes to look away from the dim light coming from the lantern Colfield had left behind. Clint worked his way around to the back of the wagon and slipped one hand into the half-open door.

Before going any further, Clint took another look at what the other two were doing. Their conversation was still moving along, so Clint took the leap and stepped into the wagon.

If there was a place where someone could mix up a tonic, poisonous or otherwise, that wagon was it. The only space to move about inside was a narrow aisle that went straight down the middle. On either side were rows of shelves lined with bottles and tins of every shape, size, and color. There were so many different types of powders in there that the air put a gritty texture on the back of Clint's tongue.

Clint's heart slammed harder in his chest with every second he spent inside that wagon. It was obvious that, whoever Colfield was, he didn't even want his own guard inside his workplace. And it was even more obvious that the inside of the wagon was most definitely a workplace.

The side of the wagon that was opposite the rear door was set up with a narrow counter and several tools. There were bowls, pestles, bottles, grinders, and a small burner used to heat a container of water. At least, it looked like water. When he got close enough to smell it, Clint pulled back immediately as a bitter stench drifted into his nose.

Clint's pulse quickened a bit more as if an alarm was going off inside his brain. He couldn't hear exactly what was being said outside, but he recognized the sound of voices that were running out of wind. It wouldn't be long before Colfield came back, and Clint knew it would be best if he wasn't there to greet him.

Looking around the wagon, Clint felt very much like he did when he was sitting at the bottom of the creek. He was in over his head. The selection on the workbench didn't make any more sense, but it was obvious that one bowl in particular was Colfield's main focus.

Since he didn't know what any of the powders or tonics were, he grabbed a bottle that was almost empty from the shelf and dumped its contents onto the floor. He then took a sample of whatever it was that Colfield was working on, scraping a portion of it into the bottle. He found a small pile of corks in a drawer, stopped up the bottle, and stashed it in a pocket where it should be relatively safe.

Now that that was done, Clint worked his way back to the door at the back of the wagon. Now that the voices outside had fallen silent, that narrow aisle seemed a whole lot longer.

Clint kept one hand on his gun as he peeked outside.

Colfield and the guard were still talking, but they seemed to be thinking something over. Finally, the man with the goatee said, "Kill him. Tell Boris to make it public and messy. Ideally, Whiteoak should be there to see it. But if the opportunity presents itself, Boris should do whatever is necessary. I've got work to do and when I'm done, that hired gun will be only one of many bodies laying in the streets of that town."

Clint pressed himself flat against the door frame and slipped out of the wagon without causing the door to move more than an inch or two. When he got outside, he let the door go so he could get back to the shadow from which he'd come.

When the wagon's door creaked shut, it sounded like a set of nails dragging over a chalkboard.

Both Colfield and the guard turned to get a look, but didn't seem too concerned. All they saw was the door shifting on its hinges and a few shadows changing their shape thanks to the clouds passing by the moon.

THIRTY-TWO

Clint rode back into Piedmont like he'd been shot from the barrel of a rifle. Eclipse cut through the night like another one of the shadows enveloping the trail leading into town. When Clint got back, Piedmont was alive with activity. Most of it came from the saloon district, but a good portion of it was due to all the lawmen patrolling the streets as if there was a war going on.

Deputies recognized Clint on sight and gave him hard stares as they watched him ride by. One deputy even stood in front of him to stop his progress. It was a particularly bold move since Eclipse was still breathing heavily and chomping at the bit after his night's run.

"Where you going, Adams?" the deputy asked. "Trying to leave town?"

"Just went out to stretch my horse's legs for a bit."

"At this time of night?"

"For your information, I've already been gone and come back," Clint said impatiently. "As you can see, I'm headed for the stable right now. If you'd like to follow me, you're more than welcome."

The deputy looked at Eclipse, and then took a second to

figure out that Clint seemed to be telling the truth. Hanging his head a bit, the deputy stepped aside.

Clint wasn't in the mood for chatting with the law. Although his clothes had mostly dried out, he was still chilled to the bone thanks to his unexpected swim. The ride had been far from a waste of time, but he still didn't know exactly what he'd discovered. All he did know was that he had precious little time to waste in figuring it out.

After riding past the deputy, Clint looked around to see that another lawman was keeping track of him from the boardwalk to see where he was going. True to his word, Clint went to the stable, put Eclipse up for the night, and headed straight out again.

The deputy was out there, and stayed just long enough to see Clint emerge before turning and walking away.

Clint turned away from all the commotion and headed for the next street. No more than a few paces along the way, he heard someone rushing to catch up to him.

"Look," Clint said as he started turning around, "there's plenty more you could be doing than following me."

Even as he spoke, Clint saw it wasn't a deputy that had been rushing up to him. The man had the toughness in his face and confidence in his step that marked him as an experienced fighter. Clint wasn't in much of a mood for that either, so he drew his Colt with a move that was so quick, it was difficult to see.

The modified pistol didn't need to be cocked before it was fired, but Clint thumbed back the hammer as a warning to the gunman who was approaching him.

"You've got two seconds to explain yourself," Clint said as the metallic click still rattled ominously through the air. "After that, you might not like what happens."

The gunman stopped and his hand twitched toward his own weapon, but he knew better than to do anything more. Slowly, he spread open his hand and eased it away from his holster. "Mr. Teasley sent me to get you."

"Why? Isn't he getting enough business through his saloon?"

"It's not about that."

"What is it about then?"

The gunman shook his head. "I don't know. All I'm supposed to do is find you and bring you back to the Dollar."

"Fine," Clint said as he holstered the Colt. "But—"

As he was talking, Clint heard a rustling behind him as more boots scraped against the dirt. He turned and drew the Colt again, just as two more attackers emerged from the shadows. One of the men came at him directly and was batted away by Clint's free hand. The gunman who'd been talking to Clint moments ago rushed in to attack Clint from behind with both fists.

Clint felt the blow land against his lower back, and swung his pistol around as if he meant to take the gunman's head from his shoulders. To the attackers' credit, they were fearless in the face of Clint's speed or the fact that he had his gun in hand. They just kept coming. When one was knocked back, another took his place.

All the while, men were grabbing at Clint's gun hand and sending vicious kicks or punches into his ribs and back.

But the gunmen weren't the only ones who fought like the devil. Clint absorbed every punch as if he didn't even feel it. The knuckles and knees that slammed into him only added fuel to the fire that burned inside him until he felt as if he was angry enough to run straight through hell without being stopped.

Twisting at the waist, Clint grabbed hold of the first gunman around the throat. He looped one arm under the man's chin and pulled him around as if he was wrestling with a doll. Clint kept that first gunman in front of him so he could look at the others from behind his new shield.

"Back the hell away from me or this really starts to get ugly," Clint snarled as he tightened his arm around the first gunman's throat.

The other two stopped dead in their tracks. Their knuckles were bloodied and their chests were heaving, but they seemed more confused than anything else since Clint had somehow managed to get the best of them. Suddenly, those two were shoved aside by a third man who charged forward like a bull.

Teasley took hold of each gunman by a shoulder and shoved them aside like they were two pieces of a batwing door. "What the fuck do you think you're doing in my town, Adams?" he growled.

Still holding the first gunman in a tight grip, Clint watched Teasley approach with a mix of anger and disbelief. "You'd better watch your tone, Teasley. I'm not in the mood for it."

THIRTY-THREE

Unlike the gunmen around him, Teasley barely seemed to notice the glare on Clint's face or even the gun in his hand. "I couldn't give a rat's ass what you're in the mood for. Answer my goddamn question."

By now, Clint could feel the first gunman's body going limp. After loosening his grip, he could tell that his arm was the only thing holding the gunman up. After taking his arm away, Clint let the gunman fall to the ground. The man landed in a heap; unconscious, but still breathing.

"What's the meaning of this?" Clint asked as he lowered his gun to hip level.

Teasley spit out a humorless laugh. "What's the meaning? What the hell's the meaning of *this?*" he retorted while snapping both hands out to point at Clint. "I welcome you into this town, welcome you into my place, and then you proceed to shoot the living hell out of everything until the law's worked up into such a lather that I can't even conduct my own affairs anymore!"

"Affairs, huh? Is that what you call it?"

"Say whatever you want about the way I do business," Teasley grumbled as he waved away Clint's accusing tone. "But you're the one stirring things up around here, not me.

I had everything worked out so it was good for everyone. The law was kept in line and so was the folks who bend it. Normal folks got to do what they want. It worked out just fine for everybody."

"Until they cross the line and get themselves lynched," Clint pointed out. "You're a real peacekeeper, Teasley. Ever think of running for mayor?"

Teasley's grin was as ugly as it was sarcastic. "Laugh it up, asshole. Your friend Whiteoak got what he deserved. You want to hear something funny? I was impressed at the way he got his ass out of here last time in one piece. In fact, I wasn't even going to lift another finger against him just as long as he kept out of my sight. But then he had to come sneaking back in here like some kind of goddamn snake."

"He thinks he can help with what's going on around here," Clint said.

"What are you talking about?"

"The folks that are sick. Whiteoak says they were poisoned and that you had something to do with it."

Teasley recoiled at the sound of that and glanced at the two gunmen, who'd seen fit to stay where they'd been shoved. "I'm poisoning people? And what bit of simpleminded reasoning brought him to that conclusion?"

"Let's face it," Clint said. "You strike me as the sort who wouldn't be above putting someone into the ground if they got on your bad side. The Silver Dollar is pretty successful and that takes a lot of hard work. Are you telling me you did all that without getting your hands dirty?"

Once again ignoring the gun in Clint's hand, Teasley stepped right up to him and looked him straight in the eye. "You're damn right I work hard and you're damn right I got my hands plenty dirty. And you're also damn right about how I deal with men who try to take away what I got.

"You know how I deal with them, Adams? I come straight at them like a nightmare or I make an example out of them. Your friend Whiteoak bilked my place out of thousands in gambling money, and his partners milked plenty of locals in crooked games. That asshole needed to be made into an example, which is just what I did when I put the wheels in motion to getting a rope around his neck.

"Me and the law have an understanding," Teasley snarled in a quieter voice. "It may not be aboveboard, but it works out for everyone concerned and doesn't get in the way with anyone doing their job."

"Sounds like a real good system," Clint said sarcastically.

"For your information, I spent some time in jail and lost a hell of a lot in fines over that lynching, even though Whiteoak's skinny neck didn't get stretched. I may know how to stand on the law's blind side, but I ain't above it. That way, I still get some support from the sheriff when slick-talking snake-oil salesmen like your friend come rolling into town. It is a good system, Adams. At least, it was until you came along and started firing off that fancy gun of yours."

"And which part of that system involves trying to knock my head off my shoulders every other time I walk down the street?"

"This is a warning. What the hell else did you expect after all the trouble you've been causing?"

"And what about the time before this?"

Teasley looked around as if someone else might have been talking. Since none of his hired guns wanted to join into the conversation, he looked back at Clint and said, "I have no idea what you're talking about. Until now, I thought we were helping each other out."

"That big fellow with the missing teeth doesn't work for you?"

"If he's missing teeth, he's probably not my best friend and sure as hell wouldn't be on my payroll."

Thinking back to that jar in the Silver Dollar, Clint nodded slowly. Although he'd been fairly certain that big man wasn't one of Teasley's boys, Clint still had to be completely certain. Now he was.

"What do you know about this disease that's sending more and more folks to the doctor's office?" Clint asked.

Teasley shrugged. "Folks get sick all the time. Them sick ones make others sick. What the hell would I know about it?"

"Perhaps that some folks say you might be behind it."

"Is that so?" Teasley asked as a smile broke across his face. "Now why might that be?"

"Rumor has it that you've been known to poison the occasional person when you wanted them to disappear."

"I'm a saloon owner, Adams. Can you imagine the damage that would be done if I spiked my own liquor with poison? I might as well board up my place, burn it down, and start up a dry-goods store. Who the hell is saying things like that?"

"Probably whoever is truly behind these poisonings. By the looks of it, that's what's making these folks sick. You might want to pull whatever strings you can to get to the bottom of it."

"Oh, I will. That is, if that's really the word that's being spread around about me." This time, Teasley was the one studying Clint's face for any hint of a lie.

"It is," Clint said earnestly. "And if you're not the man behind it, I apologize."

Teasley nodded slowly. Apparently, he was satisfied by whatever he did or didn't see in Clint's eyes. "Apology accepted."

"But if you are," Clint added, "God himself won't be able to protect you from the hell I'm getting ready to raise."

Leaving those words hanging in the air like a cold fog, Clint stepped back from Teasley, holstered his gun, and walked away. One of the gunmen started after him, but was stopped by a short, barking command from his boss.

"Let him go," Teasley snapped. "We got bigger problems."

"You believe that shit he was saying?" the gunman asked.

"Yeah, because I've heard some of it before. Go back to the Dollar, pull down all our supply of liquor, and see if it's been tampered with."

"How do I know if it has?"

"See if it's been opened! Make sure it's the same shit we normally buy or if there's anything strange stuck in there. Use your head, for Christ's sake! While you're at it, start asking around to see how far these rumors have spread and where they might have come from, but do it without spreading any more."

The gunman nodded.

"I'll be back in a few hours and you'd better have some news for me," Teasley snarled.

"Where you going?"

"To see the sheriff. Considering what I'm paying him, he at least owes me some insight into this shit storm."

THIRTY-FOUR

Clint had to knock a few times on Jenny's door before he got an answer. Even then, it was hard for him to see much more than a bit of movement through the narrow crack that appeared. Before he was forced to announce himself, the door came open as if a ghost had done it.

"It's just me," Clint announced as he walked in.

Henry Whiteoak appeared from where he was hiding behind the door and quickly shut it. "I know it's you, Clint. That's why I opened it at all. I've made something of an important discovery."

"So have I."

Ignoring Clint's reply completely, Whiteoak started talking in an excited chatter. "It seems as if Josh stumbled upon something useful after all! Remember those things you got from the doctor's office? Well, Jenny found something inside that didn't belong. And inside that, there was something else entirely!"

"What was it?" Clint asked.

"Part of a compound. A very rare part, actually, that would be used in some kind of antitoxin. But until I know what the actual toxin is, there's no way for me to narrow it down to any less than a dozen or so possibilities. Remember, whatever is being used is probably something exotic or something brewed up specially, so I can't exactly continue without . . ." Whiteoak's eyes narrowed on something Clint had taken from his pocket and was now showing him. "What's that?"

Holding out the bottle he'd taken from Colfield's wagon, Clint said, "I'm hoping it's the poison we've been looking for."

"Seriously? Where did you find it?"

"It was in a wagon just outside of—" But Clint was cut short as Whiteoak anxiously took the bottle from him and started examining it.

At first, Whiteoak held the bottle close to a lantern so he could get a look at the powder inside. He started shaking the bottle, watching the powder float inside it, and then finally started removing the cork.

"You might want to be careful, Henry," Clint warned. "If that's poison . . ."

Silencing Clint with a glare, Whiteoak said, "I am the professional here, thank you very much. I believe I know how to handle toxic substances."

Clint held up his hands and shut his mouth. Just to be safe, he also took a few steps back before Whiteoak took the cork from the bottle.

Whiteoak took out the cork, held the bottle under his nose and then sniffed it like a rabbit would sniff a piece of cabbage. Almost immediately, his eyes started blinking and tears formed in their corners. His body wobbled a bit as though he was about to pass out, but he managed to move the bottle away from his nose and take a few clear breaths before he fell over.

"It's . . . ah . . . definitely toxic," Whiteoak said as he quickly tried to regain his composure. "Where did you say you found this?"

Now that Whiteoak was listening, Clint went through a quick account of where he'd gotten the sample and who had been mixing it. It didn't take many of his observational skills for Clint to see that plenty of what he said was having an impact on Whiteoak.

"Do you know anyone named Colfield?" Clint asked once he was done with his story.

"Did you say Colfield?" Jenny asked as she opened the door and walked inside.

Clint nodded to her as she made her entrance. "I did. Where have you been?"

"Just splashing some water on my face. I brought some back for anyone else who might need it," she said, holding up a small basin full of water.

"Where'd you get that?"

Looking down at the water, Jenny looked back at Clint and said, "The creek. What's wrong with you, Clint? Where have you been?"

"He's been on a little adventure," Whiteoak said. "And he even thought to bring me a present."

"Is that why he's so suspicious?"

"Not suspicious of you," Clint said as he stepped up to Jenny. "But I am suspicious of what you've got there. Mind if I take it?"

"Help yourself."

Clint took the basin and swirled the water around. It appeared to be just as clear and cold as the water he'd been submerged in earlier. Other than that, there wasn't much more for him to see. "Henry, would you be able to tell if this water's poisoned or not?"

Whiteoak thought for a moment and then grudgingly shrugged. "Once I know what this is . . . perhaps."

"Then take it and do what you can."

"What's this about, Clint?" Jenny asked. "What's going on? First the deputies start patrolling the streets with their guns drawn, and now you start acting as if you think I did something wrong."

"I'll tell you all about it the moment we have some

time," Clint promised her. "First, we need to make sure I brought back something that might be able to keep anyone else from getting sick."

Whiteoak cleared his throat so he could get Clint's attention. "Actually, I might not be able to do much with this," he said while holding up the bottle. "My own equipment is in my wagon and my wagon isn't even in this town."

Clint's first thought was to grab Whiteoak, toss him onto Eclipse's back, and let the Darley Arabian run like the wind all the way back to where they'd left Whiteoak's wagon. But then something else came to mind, which would be a whole lot easier.

"Do you think a doctor would have the equipment you need?" Clint asked.

Whiteoak nodded. "Probably. If not, he'd certainly know where to find it. But I'm not exactly on good terms with the medical community, not to mention the locals around here."

"I might know someone who can help us out in that regard."

THIRTY-FIVE

Clint, Jenny, and Whiteoak walked quickly down the streets while trying to steer clear of the deputies. Since Dr. Chase's office wasn't too close to the saloon district, the crowds thinned out fairly well as the trio got closer to their destination. Just in case, however, Whiteoak wore his rumpled clothes and oversized hat to hide himself as much as possible.

They got to the office without incident. In fact, most locals were doing their best to steer clear of that place since it was filling up with more and more patients. Rumors of infection were spreading even quicker than the supposed disease.

Clint rapped on the door, but didn't hear anyone coming to answer it. He knocked again, and was surprised to see it pulled open by a man in his early sixties who was so thin that his steps had barely even made a sound.

The man who'd opened the door had angular features and was bald except for a thinning ring of gray hair that started behind one ear and wrapped around to the other. The scowl on his face didn't seem to have much to do with the narrow spectacles perched upon the end of his nose. Instead, the sour expression seemed expressly focused upon the people he'd found on his doorstep "What do you three want?" the old man asked.

"We'd like to come in and have a word with the doctor," Clint said.

"I'm busy. In case you didn't know, there's an epidemic going on."

Whiteoak looked up and raised a finger. "Actually, it's more of a poisoning."

"What?" the old man snapped. "Who are you? Oh, never mind. Just go away."

The door started to slam shut, but Clint stopped it with his foot. He was surprised at how much strength the old-timer had behind his effort to slam the door. "We need to speak to the doctor."

"I am Dr. Chase," the old man snapped. "Now get out of here before I have the sheriff remove you."

"My friend here is serious about the poisoning," Clint explained. "We can prove it."

"That's a lie. That's just some line of bullshit being spread around town meant to cause trouble. I've been a doctor for thirty years and I've never seen a disease this stubborn, so just leave me be before someone dies because I was out here talking to you."

"It's not a disease, sir," Whiteoak insisted.

"Just go."

But Clint wouldn't let the door shut. Before Dr. Chase could put even more force behind his effort, Clint grabbed hold of the edge of the door to keep it from moving. "Is Dorothy here?"

"Dorothy's just a nurse. What the hell do you want from her?"

"She knows me, Doctor. Please just—"

"Fine, fine," Chase grumbled as he turned his back on the door. "You two can talk all you want, but if she needs to

come to my aid, then you'll have to leave. And if she
doesn't know you, I'll have the sheriff throw you in jail for
impeding my progress in this emergency."

Clint, Jenny, and Whiteoak were following Chase into
his office as the doctor kept spouting off more threats and
insults. Neither of the three were listening to Chase, so
they weren't offended by anything the old man said. When
Clint saw Dorothy's face, he felt like he'd seen the sun
break through a thick bank of clouds.

"You know these people?" Chase asked the nurse.

Dorothy nodded and came forward to smile at Clint. "I
sure do. This fine gentleman was here—"

"Good. Whatever. Say what you need to say and be
done with it. There's some patients that need cleaning."
With that, Dr. Chase turned his back on all four of them
and stomped back into the larger room where the patients
were lying on their cots.

"He's a friendly sort," Jenny said under her breath.

Dorothy shook her head dismissively. "You should see
him when he's not feeling so well. Anyway, what brings
you back here, Clint? We are awfully busy."

"This is an associate of mine," Clint replied while
pointing toward Whiteoak. "He thinks he may be able to
help with this whole situation."

Dorothy's eyes lit up and she smiled at Whiteoak. "Really? Are you a doctor as well?"

Before Clint could explain, Whiteoak extended his hand
and spoke in a voice brimming with confidence. "I am well
studied in pharmacology and the preparation of herbs and
medicines of all kinds. My years of experience and professional expertise leads me to believe that you are dealing
with a poison. A very nasty poison, in fact."

Although she didn't seem to be completely taken in by
Whiteoak's pitch, Dorothy did show interest. "I've heard
such things from others, but there wasn't any proof."

"I have the proof right here," Whiteoak said as he held

up the bottle and presented it dramatically. "All I need is the proper equipment to dissect the toxin and devise a way to counteract it."

Without batting an eye, Dorothy said, "You mean you need to figure out an antidote?"

"Well put, my lady."

She let out an aggravated breath the moment she glanced in Dr. Chase's direction. "Dr. Chase has the proper things needed to mix up certain medicines, but normally I'd say you'd need his permission to use them." She took a heavy breath and added, "But the doctor doesn't really use any of that equipment since he insists that most anything can be cured with a little know-how and simple medicines. Funny how he started talking like that once he realized he just didn't know how to mix up much of anything."

"This really could be important, Dorothy," Clint said.

"All right then. Everything he's got is back there," Dorothy said while pointing to a small room nearby. "Just keep quiet and Dr. Chase probably won't know you're even there. He truly is quite busy."

"Thank you so much," Clint said. "Whatever I can do to repay you, consider it done."

"If this does help this epidemic or whatever it is, that'll be all the thanks I need."

THIRTY-SIX

Once Whiteoak got a look at the bottles, burners, mixers, and such in the doctor's small supply room, he was like a kid in a candy store. Clint and Jenny left him with Colfield's powder as well as the water from the creek, and then walked to the front door.

"That Dr. Chase is really something," Jenny said as she and Clint let themselves out.

"Seems like Dorothy knows how to keep him in line. No matter how difficult the man is, I still wish I could do more to help back there."

"Those folks need a cure," Jenny said simply. "Nothing much else will do any good. From what I heard, that stuff you found might have been just what Henry needed."

"You made a pretty good discovery yourself."

Jenny shrugged. "It wasn't much."

"Looks like the deputies are getting bored," Clint said as they walked down the street. "I'll bet Teasley's got plenty of men picking up the slack, though."

"So he's not the one behind all of this?"

"I don't think so. By the looks of it, the one responsible for that poison is awfully fond of setting up other folks for a fall. Men like Teasley tend to pick up a lot of enemies,

144

but I don't think he's the sort to poison anyone. He favors a more direct approach."

"I can attest to that," Jenny said. "Henry and I were almost directly hurt or killed by Teasley a few times once he caught on to what we were doing. I thought for certain he'd poisoned at least one or two of his partners sometime ago."

"Even if he did, it's an awfully big stretch for him to start poisoning random folks." Clint shook his head decisively. "No, Teasley's not the man we're after. He may be crooked and he may hire some dangerous men, but he's got no reason to do any of this. He was too angry at the results and too frustrated at what's been happening."

"That puts him in the same boat as the rest of us."

"Exactly."

"But if he didn't do it, then who did?" she asked. "This man Colfield?"

"If that stuff I found is the poison we're after, then he's definitely our man. Either that, or he's working for the culprit. Do you know who Colfield is?"

Jenny looked down at her feet and shoved her hands into her pockets. "We crossed his path once or twice," she said. "But it wasn't much of anything to talk about."

"Who is he?"

"A man in Henry's line of work. He seems to know a bit more about chemistry and all that, but he uses it to supplement his income in ways that Henry never even considered."

"He cooks up drugs?"

Jenny nodded. "Brews up opium more ways than I ever knew it could be. He made some sort of peyote that drove a few men right out of their skulls. Last time I saw him, he was getting rich selling a stronger kind of absinthe to high-society folks."

"Why would he poison people like this?" Clint asked.

She shook her head. "I haven't any idea. Even when I heard you mention his name, nothing indicated that it was even the same man. The Professor Colfield I knew was competition for Henry as far as selling tonics and such, but he was never a murderer."

"Did Whiteoak get on his bad side?"

Jenny gave Clint a look as if she was amazed he even had to ask that question. "Henry got on the bad side of anyone who tried to compete with him. That's how everyone in this line of work operates. It's not like they can just both open up for business on different sides of town. One man like Henry is lucky if he can ride in, make some money, and ride out again before he's run out on a rail. Two men like him in the same place calls down all sorts of thunder."

"Well, Colfield's definitely up to something now."

Just as Clint said that, Whiteoak came outside to join them. His shirtsleeves were rolled up past his elbows. Between his rumpled appearance and the sweat on his brow, one might have thought he'd just run several miles to get to the spot where Clint was standing.

"Dr. Chase has everything I need in there," Whiteoak said excitedly. "I should have some answers before too long."

"How long exactly?" Clint asked.

"A few hours. Maybe by morning."

"No sooner than that?"

"These things take time if you want them done right," Whiteoak explained. "I can whip up a concoction for you in half the time, but this is much harder. This is essentially stripping one down, and I'm doing a whole lot of trial and error here."

"Have you found out anything yet?"

"That powder you brought is definitely poison," Whiteoak said. "And the powder Jenny found definitely reacts to it."

"What about the water from the creek?" Clint asked. "Is that poisoned?"

"I don't know. I still need to figure out more of what that stuff is before I can test for it."

Clint looked Whiteoak straight in the eye and asked, "Will you really be able to figure this out, Henry? We don't have much time to waste."

Without blinking or tripping over a single word, Whiteoak replied, "This is why I wanted to come back here, Clint. If I didn't think I could do anything about this, I would have just headed to a much safer neck of the woods."

"All right then. What else do you need from me?"

"Right now . . . nothing. I just need time to work, but I won't have anything useful at least until morning."

Clint nodded and looked over at Jenny. "Since he's got plenty to do, how about we pay our respects to Professor Colfield?"

THIRTY-SEVEN

Now that he knew exactly where to go, Clint was able to get back to the spot where he'd fallen into the creek in no time at all. He and Jenny bolted from town, and didn't stop until their horses' hooves started kicking up chunks of wet clay.

Clint motioned for them to slow down so they could pay a little more attention to their surroundings. He told her about everything he'd seen before they'd left, so Clint didn't have to say a word along the way. Now that they were there, they didn't have to break their silence as they dismounted and approached the wagon on foot.

So far, Clint had yet to see a trace of any guards patrolling the area. He didn't even see any movement apart from the shadows and pale light from the moon creeping over the ground. Clint had no problem recognizing the spot where he'd crossed the creek. Finding that spot wasn't much help, however, since the only thing there was water and more clay.

"It was right there," Clint whispered.

Flinching a bit at the sound of Clint's voice, Jenny responded as softly as she could. "What was?"

"The wagon. It was right in that spot across the creek."

Abandoning a good amount of his effort to stay quiet, Clint stood up straight and started walking across the creek. When he saw Jenny headed for the same spot he'd used the first time, he quickly warned her. "Not there. It's tricky in spots."

"I know," she said, while stepping a bit to one side. "I can feel a drop-off right over here. Don't you think I've crossed a creek before?"

Since he hadn't told her about his embarrassing swim, Clint decided to keep it that way and avoid the ribbing that would surely follow. He met up with Jenny on the proper side of the creek and drew his pistol. Jenny followed suit and gazed around in all directions.

Clint hunkered down and ran his fingers over a fresh set of deep ruts in the clay. "This is the spot all right. It looks like they packed up the wagon and moved on."

"That clay should come in handy right about now. Let's get the horses."

In a matter of minutes, they were saddled up and riding along the side of the creek. The wagon's ruts were easy enough to follow in the areas packed with clay, but were swallowed up whenever they ventured away from the creek and into the brush. Before too long, the ruts veered off and led into bushes that were so tangled, it was hard to see which ones had been crushed by a passing wagon and which had been torn down by hunters, animals, or any other sort of thing that might have gone in that direction.

Finally, Clint and Jenny had to look at each other and admit the painful truth.

"That wagon could be anywhere," Clint said. "After all the circling we've done, Colfield and whatever men he hired would have been able to dig in and pick a juicy spot for an ambush."

"So, what now? A wagon can't be that hard to find out here. Between the two of us, we could—"

"No," Clint interrupted. "Even if we find them, we've

lost the element of surprise. I thought we knew exactly where to look, which meant we could sneak up on them. Now, we'd just be stomping around trying to get lucky. It'd be easier for them to spot us coming from miles away."

"Who cares if they spot us?" Jenny said. "I can handle myself and I'm sure you can handle a few hired guns."

"That's not the point. It's Colfield I'm worried about."

She laughed under her breath and replied, "You shouldn't be worried about the Professor. I think even Henry could get the best of him in a fight."

"And what happens if he is poisoning folks through the creek?" Clint asked. "What if he sees us coming and decides to hurry up and dump whatever he's got left into the water?"

"You don't know the creek is poisoned yet."

"If he's not poisoning the creek now, he might threaten to do that if we don't let him go. There's too many folks sick and dying right now for me to risk something like that."

It was plain to see that she didn't like it, but Jenny finally started to nod. "You're right," she admitted. "I just don't much like waiting around."

"Neither do I, but we don't have much choice. Whenever Whiteoak is finished with what he's doing, he's going to need someone backing him up."

"Backing him up for what?"

"Even if it's taking what he's found out to someone other than Dorothy, Whiteoak will need some help. He's not exactly trusted in that town."

Reluctantly, Jenny steered her horse back toward Piedmont. They raced back into town, put their horses into the stable, and checked in on Whiteoak before the sun started to make its presence known. All they got for their efforts was to be waved off by Whiteoak, who barely even took the time to look up from what he was doing. Luckily, Dr. Chase was still too busy with his own tasks to notice anything out of the ordinary in his office.

"I'll send word to you when I need you," Whiteoak said. "Or if I need anything. Just stop bothering me."

Clint left Whiteoak and snuck out of the doctor's office before anyone but Dorothy noticed he was even there. As he left, he saw that there were a few more patients in the larger room than the last time he'd checked.

"What's he doing in there?" Jenny asked from where she'd been waiting outside.

"Hell if I know. Whatever it is, he's busy doing it, so I'll just let him work."

"What are we supposed to do now?"

"He said he'd send someone for us, so I guess we go back to the hotel and wait."

Clint and Jenny headed down the street. The entire town of Piedmont had quieted down in the last hour or so. Instead of crawling with deputies, gunmen, gamblers, and drunks, the place was all but empty.

Instead of a town, Piedmont felt more like a graveyard.

THIRTY-EIGHT

Even though they'd been up for one hell of a long time, gone riding, running, sneaking, and even swimming, Clint and Jenny were still a long way from being able to sleep. They made it back to the hotel without saying more than a handful of words to each other. Once in their room, Clint leaned back in a chair while Jenny curled up on the bed.

Clint's eyes remained half open as he went over everything in his mind. Every time he thought back to something that had been accomplished, he remembered something else to wipe that accomplishment away.

Tracks they'd found led nowhere.

Clues to a mystery were unable to be understood.

Suspicious men suddenly seemed innocent, and the one man who seemed to be at the center of it all was still little more than a ghost.

All the while, folks were taking their last breaths and there wasn't much of anything Clint could do about it.

As much as he wanted to get some rest, Clint's thoughts just wouldn't slow down enough for him to let himself fall asleep. His eyes remained half open. His arms were crossed into a knot over his chest and his feet kept shifting and scraping against the floor.

He twitched toward his gun when he felt a hand drop onto his shoulder, but he quickly saw it was Jenny who was approaching him from the side. She'd managed to crawl out of bed and walk over to him like a cat on padded feet.

"You can't sleep either," she stated.

"Having you sneak up on me doesn't help," Clint replied.

"And having you rub your legs together like a cricket doesn't exactly do wonders for me."

Clint let out a fretful breath and shrugged. His eyes opened all the way when he felt Jenny swing one leg over him and settle onto his lap. She faced him as she lowered herself down, resting her hands on his shoulders.

"What are you doing?" Clint asked.

"If you don't know, then you must be more sleepy than I thought."

Although he sounded resistant, Clint's hands found their way onto her hips and he shifted in his chair to accommodate her. "We need to be ready to move. Whiteoak might send for us any time now."

Jenny silenced him with a gentle kiss on the lips. She followed it up with another kiss, which was harder and more urgent. Clint felt the tension inside him melt away as her lips touched his. When he opened his mouth and licked her lips, he felt an excitement explode within him that gave him a fresh burst of energy.

"Morning won't be here for a while," Jenny whispered as she writhed on top of him. "And if we stay as tightly wound as we are, we won't be any use to Henry when the time does come."

Clint's hands were busy along her sides, running up over her hips and lingering on her breasts. He could feel her nipples growing harder through her shirt. As she eased a hand between Clint's legs, she could feel him getting harder as well.

"You've got a point there," Clint said between quick, powerful kisses. "Anything it takes to stay alert."

After that, neither one of them said another word.

Jenny took a step back and pulled open her jeans so she could pull them off. Clint did the same while staying seated. He unbuckled his gun belt, and then took down his own jeans while watching Jenny strip in front of him. Seeing her naked from the waist down as she climbed back on top of him was enough to make him lose track of every one of his worries.

Gathering up the tails of her shirt, Jenny held them up as she straddled Clint's lap. She even looked down to watch her pussy accept him as Clint guided himself into her. Once she felt his rigid cock start to enter her, she lowered herself down and took every inch of him inside.

Clint leaned back in his chair and grabbed hold of Jenny's firm backside. When she leaned forward to support herself with both hands against the back of the chair, she followed the rhythm of Clint's hands as he pulled her forward and eased her back.

Every time he slid inside her, Clint could feel Jenny's pussy becoming warmer and wetter. Once she began gliding against his cock, she leaned back and let out a slow, satisfied moan. Jenny scooted forward and situated her feet against the floor. From there, she was able to wriggle her hips back and forth once she'd lowered all the way down.

Letting out a slow breath of his own, Clint opened his eyes and watched Jenny rock back and forth on top of him. Her face was completely serene as she let her hair sway to either side. He reached up to unbutton her shirt and slip his hands inside so he could cup her breasts and rub her nipples with his thumbs.

Jenny responded to that with a little smile, as if she was reacting to a dream. Taking her hands off the back of the chair, she grabbed hold of Clint's shoulders and began pumping her hips in earnest. At first, her pace was steady and eager. Then, she locked eyes with Clint and started riding him hard.

She leaned forward and stared into his eyes as Clint's hands moved down to her buttocks and grabbed her tightly. When she paused for a moment to catch her breath, Jenny felt Clint start to thrust up into her. Clutching onto him, she let her head droop forward so she could breathe directly into Clint's ear. That was more than enough to send a shiver down Clint's spine.

For the next few minutes, Jenny simply rode him in a nice, steady rhythm. When the time was right, Clint drove up into her, which pushed Jenny into a powerful climax. Her hands tightened on Clint's shoulders and she tightened around his cock. When the storm passed, she pumped her hips faster and faster until she was able to drive him to the same height where she'd just been.

When Clint exploded inside her, he felt as if his entire body was finally able to relax.

After that, neither one of them had any trouble getting some sleep.

THIRTY-NINE

It was late morning when Clint heard the footsteps rattling down the hall toward his room. Although he'd been resting, that sound snapped his eyes open and got his body moving in a flash. By the time the steps had reached his door, Clint was already opening it and taking a look outside.

"Dorothy?" Clint said as he pulled the door open all the way and lowered his gun. "What's the matter?"

The nurse's face was flushed and her breaths were coming in short gasps. Her eyes were wide and she grabbed for Clint's arm the instant she caught sight of him. "You've got to come with me. There's some trouble."

"What is it?"

"Dr. Chase found out about your friend. I tried to calm him down, but he wouldn't have any of it. They're at each other's throats and I didn't know what else to do but come and get you. Your friend told me where to look for you."

Rather than try to untangle the mess of words coming from Dorothy, Clint buckled his gun belt around his waist and dropped his Colt into the holster. Grabbing his jacket and throwing it on, he said, "Let's go."

Jenny was right at Clint's side.

• • •

Even before Clint set foot inside the doctor's office, he could hear the shouting coming from inside. When he heard glass shattering, Clint and the two women with him all raced toward the door. Inside, they found more than enough chaos to go along with the noise.

"You're a charlatan and a sneak!" Dr. Chase shouted. "I told you to get out of my office and I meant it!"

"But you don't understand!" Whiteoak shouted back. "I'm almost finished."

"Oh, you're finished all right!" Chase grabbed the first object he could find, and then cocked his arm back to throw that object at Whiteoak. His swing was stopped short when a powerful grip clamped around his wrist and held his arm in place.

Chase wheeled around to shoot a fiery glare at Clint. "Let go of me," he snarled. "Or I'll instruct the sheriff to throw you in jail right along with this one."

"Take a breath," Clint said as he pulled the thick ceramic bowl from Dr. Chase's hand. "Settle down and hear us out."

"I don't have to listen to anyone who breaks into my office, steals my supplies, and helps themselves to my things. In fact, I should have you arrested!"

As if finally noticing Clint was there, Whiteoak said, "I've figured out what kind of poison this is."

"It's not a poison!" Chase interrupted.

There was no mistaking the look that Clint gave to the doctor at that moment. Chase could either shut his mouth or deal with the consequences, and Clint didn't even have to speak for anyone to know what those consequences would be. Although Chase bit his tongue, he was shaking with the effort.

"What did you find, Henry?" Clint asked.

"The compound Jenny discovered in that locket is a

spice used by the Chinese as a way to . . ." He trailed off
when he already felt his audience slipping away. "The important thing is that this powder only reacts to a few different things. Those things, in turn, only react to a few other
things and so on. I eventually narrowed it down until I realized what poison was being used here."

"That sounds really complicated," Clint said, hoping
that Whiteoak wasn't merely talking bullshit.

But Whiteoak was too excited to bluff. On the contrary,
he shrugged dismissively when he said, "It's simple
chemistry."

"All right. So what is it?"

Getting excited again, Whiteoak said, "It's a mix of this
Chinese formula with a few venoms. The Chinese stuff is
used to help other things get into your blood. Sort of like a
shoehorn."

As odd as the analogy was, Clint didn't have any trouble
understanding it.

"It also masks flavor and, to some degree, smell,"
Whiteoak continued.

"And isn't that convenient?" Chase grunted. "This
sounds like another bullshit sales pitch explaining why we
should buy something you can't see, taste, or smell."

"Is that what this is, Henry?" Clint asked.

"Not hardly. I am very familiar with these things, and so
is Professor Colfield. I'm sure Jenny has told you about
him by now."

Clint nodded, and Dr. Chase rolled his eyes.

"Actually, it's not surprising that the good doctor here
isn't familiar with this sort of thing," Whiteoak said. "It's
mainly something used in a, shall we say, less than legal
capacity. Men who make certain narcotics use the mixture
to lace in other chemicals designed to give their particular
creations a different flavor. Just a way for men like Professor Colfield to stay competitive."

"Competitive with other fiends like yourself," Dr. Chase pointed out.

Whiteoak didn't admit to that, but he looked away with a hint of shame in his eyes. Finally, he muttered, "Not for a very long time."

"Just like I thought," Chase said smugly. "You're probably behind this whole thing or partners with the man who is."

"And you're probably a man who's too arrogant to admit when he's wrong," Whiteoak shot back. "You've been running around here for days trying to treat these folks for something they don't have just because you don't want to contradict your first diagnosis. Well, you are wrong, Doctor. It happens to the best of us. At least I'm able to think along a different line. If you were any sort of real scientist, you'd welcome any help you could get to save these folks instead of beating your head against the same goddamn wall! The fact that you're not even listening to me right now only proves what a piss-poor doctor you truly are."

Clint nodded without doubting Whiteoak's words in the least. "Is there a way for you to see if that creek water is laced with that stuff?"

Whiteoak shifted his eyes to Clint and nodded warily. "It's diluted, but yeah. It's in there."

"Now, more importantly, can you do anything about it?"

"Most definitely," Whiteoak said. "Now that I know what it is, I was able to mix up an antidote for it. Of course, there's the possibility that there's some venoms in the mix that I don't know about, but I was able to put something together that can get these sick folks back on track."

Chase let out a short grunt of a laugh. "I can't believe you people are seriously considering this. I mean, listening to a known cheat and swindler when it comes to a matter of life and death. That's practically sealing these people's fates."

Clint squared off with the doctor and said, "Fine, then let me know what your idea is. As far as I can see, those people are still laying on their cots and dying. In fact, it looks like there's more of them now."

Doctor Chase gritted his teeth and balled up his fists. "You know nothing about practicing medicine."

"That's true. But from where I'm standing, that swindler has a better grasp on what's going on here than you."

"He has no proof to back up these wild theories."

"What about it, Henry?" Clint asked. "Can you make sure that antidote works?"

"Well, I did administer it to one of the patients."

"What!" Chase roared.

"I told him my theories and what I was doing and he agreed to try it out voluntarily."

"This is outrageous! If that man is hurt, I'll see to it that you are hung from the highest pole in this state!"

Clint stepped between the doctor and Whiteoak, focusing his attention on the latter. "How's the patient doing?"

Pointing to the cot closest to the room where he'd been working, Whiteoak said, "Ask him for yourself."

Everyone turned to look at that patient, finding that he was the only one in that room who was actually sitting up and had some color returning to his face. When he saw he was being watched, the patient grinned weakly and gave them a wave.

"That's good enough for me," Clint said. "Henry, whip up as much of that stuff as you can and give me as much as you can spare of what you've already got."

"Will do."

"Jenny, you and I are going to search every inch of that creek. If Professor Colfield is poisoning the water, he's going to have to stay close to it."

Before Jenny could say anything, Dr. Chase fumed, "I'm notifying the law about this. You'll be a wanted man before you can get to your horse."

"Do your worst, Doc."

FORTY

True to his word, Dr. Chase rounded up the sheriff within moments after Clint and Jenny left his office. Although this wasn't foremost on Clint's mind, it was difficult not to spot the small posse that was there to greet him when he and Jenny were leading their horses out of the stable.

"What's this I hear about you being involved with this epidemic, Adams?" Sheriff Morton asked as he and his men stepped forward.

"If you mean we're involved in trying to end it, then yeah, we're involved all the way up to our necks."

The sheriff looked over at Dr. Chase, who was standing nearby and shaking his head.

"That's not what I mean," Morton said. "If you're stirring things up to make them worse or to keep the doctor from doing his job, I'll have to take you in. It's a matter of public health."

"If you're so concerned about public health," Clint said as he climbed into Eclipse's saddle, "then you should get yourself another town doctor."

Morton and his deputies fanned out. At one nod from the sheriff, the deputies drew their guns and held them at the ready.

"Don't make me do this, Adams," Morton said.

"Do what? We're going out for a ride."

"You intend on spreading that concoction into our drinking water and I can't allow that."

Clint looked over at Dr. Chase and saw the old man grinning smugly right back at him. "Look, Sheriff. If you'd let me explain—"

"No need to explain anything, Adams," came a gruff voice from the other side of the street. "If you've got some important things to do, just go ahead and do them."

Although Clint and Jenny strained their necks to see who was coming, none of the lawmen had to go through so much trouble.

Without taking his eyes from Clint, Sheriff Morton said, "Get back to your saloon, Teasley. This doesn't concern you."

"On the contrary, I believe it does. Anything that affects the drinking water of this town affects a man like myself very much. Especially with me being so involved in the distribution of so many things that go into folks' mouths around here." Teasley grinned at that, and the men who walked up to stand with him laughed as well.

"I told you to get out of here."

When Teasley responded to the sheriff this time, there wasn't one bit of humor in his voice. "And I told you to leave him be."

Sheriff Morton shifted on his feet so he could get a look at the saloon owner. "What the hell are you doing, Cal? Do you even know what's going on here?"

"Everyone in town knows what's going on. We're the ones getting sick."

"Then you should know what a danger this man and especially that Whiteoak fellow is posing. You remember Whiteoak, don't you? That asshole who stole from you and swindled countless others in this town alone?"

"Whiteoak may be an asshole, but he knows a lot about

mixing tonics," Teasley replied. "I've dealt with him long enough to know that. If he wants to lend a hand with our epidemic, I say we let him."

"What about Dr. Chase?" Morton asked. "You just going to write him off?"

"Chase could barely saw a leg off during the War Between the States. I'd say the subtleties of this situation are way beyond him. If it wasn't, this shit would've been cleared up by now, wouldn't it?"

Clint and Jenny kept quiet while the two bickered. Surprisingly enough, the edge in the sheriff's voice seemed a bit duller than it had been a few moments ago.

"You're willing to go to the line for these people?" Morton asked.

"My saloon won't sell no liquor in a town full of dead people, Sheriff. Besides, I think you owe me a few favors, so I'd appreciate it if you let my friend Adams do what he needs to do."

Sheriff Morton winced at that and glanced around nervously. "This is worth a few more favors besides," he said.

"How about you do this or that weekly envelope of favors you get just stops coming?"

Letting out a breath, Morton said, "Fine, Teasley. But if this turns out bad, you're answering for it."

"Fair enough."

Sheriff Morton rounded up his men and left.

"All right, then," Teasley said with a self-satisfied grin. "You need any backup for this little job, Adams?"

FORTY-ONE

Clint, Jenny, and half a dozen of Teasley's hired guns rode out of Piedmont like a stampede. They fanned out and covered the creek on both sides as they thundered along the winding flow of water. Clint still couldn't get his mind around the fact that Teasley was helping him. Apparently, Clint wasn't the only one.

"Do you seriously trust these men?" Jenny asked.

"I didn't at first, but they don't have any reason to make me doubt them."

"How about the fact that they work for Teasley?"

"Teasley's not behind this."

"Maybe not, but he's behind plenty of other things. Like trying to hang Henry, for one."

"Henry's still alive. You ask me, he needs to get a close call every so often to keep him honest. Well, close to honest."

"I still don't like it," Jenny muttered.

"They're just muscle, eyes, and ears. Right now, I'll take help from anywhere I can get it. Once this poison is gone, we can iron out the rest of the details."

"Stop right here," she said.

Clint shook his head and said, "I told you. We're using these men just to help us find that wagon."

"I did find the wagon. Stop right here!"

Pulling back on his reins brought Eclipse to a stop. Clint dug his spyglass from the saddlebag and looked in the direction Jenny was pointing. Even with the naked eye, he could see the blocky shape that didn't quite blend in with the rest of the terrain. Sure enough, once he looked through the spyglass, Clint saw the narrow window in the side of the wagon he was after.

"That's it all right," Clint said as he put the spyglass back. He then let out a short, crisp whistle intended to catch the attention of the hired guns in his vicinity. A few men rushed over to him.

"You see something?" one of the gunmen asked.

Clint pointed toward the wagon. "Right over there. I didn't see anyone around it, but I know the Professor has guards walking the area."

"You want me to take some men and hunt down them guards?"

"It'd be quicker if you just flush them out the easy way. You think you can do that without getting shot?"

"We ain't idiots, Adams," the gunman said with a sour look on his face.

"I didn't mean it like that. I just don't want you to rush in and get yourselves killed just to clear the way for me."

The gunman grinned and slapped Clint on the shoulder. "Don't worry about it. This is what we do." With that, the gunman snapped his reins, rode away from the creek, and motioned for the other men to follow. They were more than willing to take orders from him than Clint, so they thundered off and then started firing their guns in the air.

Clint watched them go and shook his head. "I was hoping to give them a few suggestions, but that'll do."

"It sure will," Jenny said while nodding toward the wagon. "Take a look."

Clint looked in that direction again and saw three horses appear from behind a thick cluster of bushes and take off after the rampaging gunmen. Soon, another rider appeared from behind the wagon to join the rest.

"I stand corrected," Clint said with a smirk. "Let's see if we can get over there without drawing so much attention."

He snapped his reins and got Eclipse moving at well under full speed. Jenny followed closely, and even the two of their horses combined didn't make enough noise to be noticed over the chaos being unleashed by Teasley's men.

The Darley Arabian nearly cleared the creek in one jump, and Clint swung down from the saddle as soon as hooves hit the clay. With a swat on the stallion's rump, he got Eclipse moving in another direction and headed toward the wagon.

Jenny was close behind him, and they both circled around to the side of the wagon that was facing away from the growing commotion of yelps and gunshots. As soon as Clint had the wagon in his sight, he saw the door at the back of it fly open and the familiar man with the goatee hurry outside.

For a man who looked to be in his fifties, Professor Colfield moved pretty well. Even with his arms wrapped around several large tin canisters, he rushed to the creek without spilling anything from a single one of them. He almost made it to the water before a gunshot blasted through the air and a bullet punched into the ground at his feet.

"That'll be far enough," Clint said.

Colfield turned to look at Clint. When he saw him, he nodded as if bidding him a friendly hello. "Mr. Adams. You're a hard man to track down."

"Yeah. I've been busy. By the looks of it, so have you."

Colfield tightened his grip on the canisters and nodded once. "A man doesn't get rich by sitting idle."

"He also doesn't get rich by killing innocent people."

"Ah. There's where you're wrong. A man can get quite rich that way. At least, if he has connections in the right places."

Clint stepped forward with Jenny right beside him. Both of them had their guns aimed at Colfield, but that didn't stop him from backing away from them while still angling toward the creek.

"Trying to poison the water a little further upstream?" Clint asked. "I was hoping you hadn't gotten to that yet. Especially since my horse and I happened to swallow more than our share the other night."

"Don't shit where you sleep," Colfield said. "Isn't that the way the saying goes?"

Clint nodded. "You'll be sleeping in jail tonight. After that, you might just be sleeping underground once you stand trial for what you've done."

Colfield shook his head. "You come near me, and I'll dump all of this into the creek. I'd rather not waste so much of it, but I will unless you back off and let me pass."

As the Professor leaned toward the creek, Clint glanced toward Piedmont in the distance. He also knew well enough there were at least two other towns farther down the creek that had yet to be touched by the poison.

It wasn't often that so many lives could be packed into a few tin canisters held in the arms of a madman.

FORTY-TWO

"Why are you doing this?" Jenny asked. "Are you crazy?"

"Not hardly. Opium and peyote will only take you so far. I found a man who trades in weapons of all kinds and he'll pay handsomely for something like this," Colfield explained. Hugging the canisters to himself, he asked, "You know what this is? It's a town killer. It can win wars, clear out unwanted squatters from valuable property, eradicate the herds of rival ranchers. The possibilities are all there and it's untraceable! The good doctor in Piedmont didn't have the first notion of what was going on."

"You were found out eventually," Clint said. "Which brought us to this very spot."

"I only put a small amount in the waters directly outside that town," Colfield said proudly. "And that was before I'd perfected the formula. I've been working on it day and night and the results I've gotten have been more than enough to impress my potential investors. Even now, they're in a bidding war to see who'll get exclusive rights to my formula."

"Jesus Christ," Clint said. "Jenny's right. You are crazy."

The shooting echoed from where Teasley's hired guns were locking horns with the guards they'd found. As the sounds of the fight kept going, Clint started to feel worse and worse about this whole thing. Either Teasley's men were terrible shots, or there were a whole lot more of Colfield's men than Clint had thought.

But Colfield didn't seem to notice any of that. In fact, he barely even took notice of Clint and Jenny as his eyes were drawn more and more to the creek. "What I've got here is enough to kill every living thing in that town, even if a small fraction of it makes it there. But it'll wipe out at least two or maybe three other towns between here and the ocean. My God. That will make national headlines."

Clint stepped forward quickly. "That's it. You just talked yourself into one hell of a headache."

But before Clint could get within arm's reach of the Professor or even raise his gun to take a shot, he was knocked clean off his feet by what felt like a charging bull.

Clint had just heard the sound of heavy footsteps when he felt something slam into his ribs. When he blinked again, he was on his back with one arm touching the edge of the creek. The sky stretched out in front of him, but was soon eclipsed by a big, ugly face displaying a gap-toothed smile.

"I've been looking all over for you," Boris said. "But I knew you weren't gonna get away."

Jenny raced up to come to Clint's aid, but she was swatted away with a viciously quick backhand and sent sprawling to the ground. After shaking her head to clear away some of the cobwebs, she realized her gun was no longer in her hand. The only problem was that she didn't even know which way it had gone.

Clint's mind screamed at him to hit the big man, kick him, do anything at all to answer the initial blow that had taken him off his feet. But when his body tried to carry out any of those orders, all it could do was feel a whole world of pain.

All the breath had been stolen from Clint's lungs when

he'd been hit, making it difficult for him to do much more than roll over. Luckily, he was able to do that much since that allowed him to dodge the huge boot that slammed down in the spot where his head had been a moment ago.

Boris kept grinning and nodded as he stomped a hole in the ground. Like a giant crushing a small village, he lifted his other foot, swung it forward, and slammed that one downward toward the side of Clint's head.

It was pure survival instinct that kept Clint rolling so he could avoid the second boot falling down on him. He stopped quickly on his side, facing Boris, and reached out to grab hold of the bigger man's foot. As soon as he had a solid grip, Clint put all his muscle behind a single twist.

Letting out a surprised shout, Boris hopped to try and maintain his balance, but was quickly brought down. Somehow, the big man got one knee beneath him before toppling over completely. He balled up one giant fist and took a swing at Clint's jaw. As the shot landed, he reached behind his back with his other hand to take out a short, thick club that was still stained by a deputy's blood.

Clint could no longer hear the gunshots in the distance. He couldn't see Colfield trying to kill countless people with the venom he'd created. All he could hear was the impact of fists against his face and the rush of blood through his veins. All he could see was Boris coming at him like a bad dream with death gleaming in his eyes.

Saving those towns from Colfield's poison seemed impossible.

Clint was starting to wonder if he could save himself.

FORTY-THREE

The moment she saw Boris take Clint off his feet, Jenny held onto one single thought: Clint can handle himself. That thought was the only thing that allowed her to turn away from him so she could try to do something about Professor Colfield as he set his sights upon the creek.

Colfield staggered forward under the weight of the canisters he was holding. All the while, his eyes were wide at the prospect of emptying those canisters just to see what kind of havoc his creation would unleash.

"Don't!" she screamed as she ran forward. It was the only thing she could think of to keep Colfield from taking another step.

Somehow, it worked.

Colfield stopped and turned to look at her. His eyes were glazed over and he spoke in a wheezing, breathless voice. "There's nothing you can do!"

"The hell there isn't!" Jenny replied as she dug her feet into the ground and ran faster than she ever thought she could.

She made it to Colfield and managed to knock him away from the creek. Her heart jumped up to the back of her throat, however, when she saw him stagger back and fall down with his canisters still in hand. Colfield hit the hard ground and dropped all but one of the canisters. One of those that he dropped broke open on impact and spilled its poison onto the ground.

Jenny could smell the acrid mixture of chemicals that suddenly filled the air. It made her throat itch and her stomach churn after just a few breaths, so she reflexively shut her mouth and held onto the breath that she'd already taken.

"No!" Colfield shouted as he scrambled to scoop the powdery substance back into its container. After a few attempts, he gave up on trying to save the poison and turned a vengeful glare toward Jenny. "Do you know how much money you just cost me?"

Colfield struggled to get to his feet, but his legs were already more than a little unsteady beneath him. Even so, he was determined to get up again just so he could wrap his hands around Jenny's throat. That much was obvious by the fire in his eyes.

Jenny took another few steps and lowered her shoulder as she charged Colfield. When she plowed into him, the impact was enough to knock him back a step or two, but that was about it.

"You stupid bitch!" Colfield snarled. "That's my life's work you just dumped!" As he said that, Colfield balled up his fist and pounded it against Jenny's face.

The punch landed solidly on her cheek, snapping her head to one side and sending a wave of black through her eyes. Although she'd been in a few scrapes with angry gamblers and a couple of belligerent drunks, she'd never been on the receiving end of a straight punch from a man.

After a quick breath, the fog lifted from behind her eyes and Jenny realized that only a second or so had ticked by. Although her face was stinging with pain, Jenny managed to grit her teeth and show Colfield a lopsided grin.

"You hit like a little girl, Professor."

Hearing those words after everything else that had just happened was enough for Colfield to drop the last canister he was holding, turn his back to the creek, and charge at Jenny with both fists swinging. His first swing was aimed at her chin and designed to separate her head from her shoulders.

Jenny's blood was flowing like firewater and she saw that swing coming from a mile away. After ducking underneath Colfield's fist, she felt another impact on her shoulder blade as he pounded on the only target he had available.

Once he felt his second blow land, Colfield followed it up with another as he beat on Jenny's back like it was a drum. The world was starting to fade around him as more and more of his senses started slipping away. Colfield recognized the tingle of the powder in his nose since he'd been working with it for so long, but this was the first time he'd been exposed to so much without even a bandanna to cover his face.

"They'll hear about what I did," Colfield said as he took another swing at Jenny. "They'll see what I did and pay any price I name. You wait and see! I'll be richer than a king!"

Jenny was getting into a good rhythm that allowed her to duck Colfield's wild punches. When she saw him go for a gun that had been kept under his belt, she knew she had to make her next move count for a lot. Her life was depending on it.

"It's too late to stop it," Colfield said as he fumbled to get his gun in his hand. After a few tries, he managed to get his finger on the trigger. "I only hope that bastard Whiteoak is dying as well. If anyone deserves it—"

Colfield was cut short as he felt cold steel plunge into his gut.

Jenny had managed to get to the knife she kept in her boot and lunge forward with every bit of strength she could muster. After burying the knife into Colfield, she was unable to do anything else before he twisted around and took the knife out of her hand.

Although he'd been able to get the knife away from Jenny, that was only because it was lodged deeply in his stomach. As his blood started to flow out of him, Colfield lost his strength in the same way he'd been losing his senses. He swayed for a moment, dropped to the ground, and then immediately started crawling for his canisters.

"They'll still . . . see," he wheezed, ". . . too late . . . to stop it."

Jenny gasped as she saw that Colfield wasn't just crawling away from her. As he got closer to his canisters, he reached out and started pushing them toward the creek. Jenny made it to him quickly, but didn't have the strength to pull Colfield away. Her gun was still nowhere to be seen and her knife was more than halfway into Colfield's belly.

Moving to the spot where Colfield was crawling, Jenny sucked in another deep breath, held it, and dropped down so one knee landed in Colfield's back. He kept trying to move and shove another canister toward the water, but suddenly felt a weight press down upon his shoulder. Soon, the weight moved to the back of his head.

Holding her breath until her lungs strained, Jenny felt her eyes tearing up as she shoved Colfield's face into the poison that he'd spilled earlier. The man had a fraction of the strength he'd had moments ago and it was fading quickly.

She held his face in the poison like she was pushing a dog's nose into its own mess. Finally, the dog stopped kicking.

FORTY-FOUR

Clint and Boris fought like two wildcats over a fresh kill. Both men were bloodied and bruised in no time at all. Clint had absorbed some vicious blows from the big man, but had managed to answer back with plenty of his own. Somehow, Boris just kept coming. More than that, his gap-toothed grin only seemed to grow.

Eventually, Clint shoved himself away so he could get some distance from the big man. Boris caught one of Clint's heels in the side of his knee, which sent him staggering back just long enough for Clint to get away. Although it had been Clint's intention to back off and find another angle of attack, he spotted something that he dearly missed lying on the ground between him and Boris.

Somewhere during the fight, Clint's modified Colt had been knocked loose. When he spotted it lying there, and while Boris was still reeling from the kick he'd taken, Clint dove with both arms outstretched toward his pistol. The feeling of his fingers wrapping around the pistol's grip was a victory in itself. Once he got a look at Boris, however, Clint felt anything but victorious.

The big man was already steady and on his feet. He was covered with scars and wounds from their previous encounters, as well as plenty more from other battles. Rather than look bloody and injured, however, Boris looked like a lion displaying his mane. He wore his scars like medals and he looked at Clint with grim determination.

"You want to use that gun?" Boris asked as he flipped open his jacket to show the gun at his own hip. "Fine. I'll be sure to wound you, though, so I can finish you off with my bare hands."

The two men circled each other, giving Clint a moment to take in his surroundings. Although the fighting in the distance was fading away, he saw that Jenny and Colfield were locked in their own struggle. As much as it pained him to do so, he took his eyes away from her and focused on Boris. He knew he wouldn't be any help to anyone if he was dead.

"You must be insane to sign on with a man like Colfield," Clint said.

Boris shrugged. "He wasn't lying about his investors. He pays me more money than I've ever seen. Even if he dies here, I'll be able to sell that poison of his and buy my own country."

"Over my dead body."

"That was the plan."

With that said, Boris reached for his gun.

Clint spotted the movement the moment it started. Even so, the big man somehow managed to clear leather before Clint could stop him. Boris was fast, but he wasn't fast enough to aim and fire before Clint lifted the Colt and squeezed his trigger.

The Colt barked once and sent a round into Boris. That was barely enough to knock the big man back a step, but not enough to keep Boris from firing. He brought up his gun and fired a round at Clint, which hissed through the air like an angry hornet.

Clint started to doubt his own senses, even as he launched himself backward and off his feet. He knew he'd hit Boris, but the big man didn't even seem to feel it. That rattled Clint more than the bullet that had nearly taken a piece out of his skull.

Boris fired again, but his shot went through the spot where Clint had been before dropping back.

Landing hard on the packed earth, Clint felt a good amount of the wind rush out of his lungs. He reflexively took a shot at Boris, even though he knew he was going to miss. As another round blazed from Boris's pistol, Clint steadied himself, took a breath, and did exactly what needed to be done.

With a quick series of efficient movements, he fired the Colt again and again while counting down the number of remaining bullets in his head. That number was down to one before he started getting to his feet. All Clint needed to see was one more movement from Boris for him to send his final bullet whipping through the air.

For a moment, Boris stood there like a statue. His head was leaning back and his chest was wet with blood. Several holes had been drilled through him by Clint's bullets, but that still wasn't enough to put Boris down.

The big man dragged his head back up and stared at Clint with the third eye that had just been punched into his forehead. Letting out a final wheeze, he dropped to his knees and slumped over. Only then did Clint allow himself to take another breath.

The air was quiet and hung heavy around him. The sounds of gunshots were gone, to be replaced by Jenny's tired voice.

"We were too late," she said.

Clint looked around at the bodies scattered near the

wagon before he caught sight of the canisters that lay broken and spilled at the edge of the creek. He forced himself to shake his head and look her straight in the eye as he replied, "It's never too late."

FORTY-FIVE

The fires crackled, filling the dark sky with an orange glow. At first, the smoke reeked with a bitter, pungent stench and had an unusual color about it. Before too long, however, the flames swallowed up Professor Colfield's wagon as well as the chemicals in and around it.

Clint had poured kerosene everywhere he saw the poison had been spilled. After lighting the match, he'd run back to Eclipse and ridden straight back into Piedmont. After visiting Whiteoak and sampling some of his antidote for themselves, Clint and Jenny rode along the creek to where the fires had joined into one, enormous blaze.

They weren't alone while watching the flames. Whiteoak was with them, and was visibly shaken when he saw Teasley and a few of his gunmen wander over to take in the sight.

"Quite a show," Teasley said. "From what I hear, Whiteoak, you're practically a hero for mixing up that antidote. Well done."

Shifting a bit closer to Clint, Whiteoak replied, "Um, thank you."

"Seriously. I think I speak for everyone in Piedmont when I say you did a fine job and we're all indebted to you."

This time, Whiteoak grinned easier and nodded. "Thanks very much."

Teasley leaned over and draped an arm around Whiteoak's shoulder. Pulling him in close, he dropped his voice to a whisper and said, "Speaking for myself, if I see your face around here again, I'll wrap a noose around it so tight that the hand of God won't be able to pull you out of it." After that, he let Whiteoak go, tipped his hat to Clint and Jenny, and then rode back into town.

"He just threatened my life," Whiteoak said.

Clint shrugged and kept watching the fire. "You did real good in coming back to set this straight, Henry. Maybe if you'd stop cheating folks out of their money, they'd be more apt to welcome you back."

"I did save their lives."

"Yes, you did. I'm proud of you and you should be proud of yourself. Isn't that enough for now?"

"I guess," Whiteoak said unconvincingly. "Do you think all of that poison is gone?"

"There won't be much left but ash after that fire dies down. Even if some does slip by, that antidote works really well. Eclipse and I took sips of that water before we knew any better and we're doing fine."

"A whole lot of that stuff was spilled," Jenny said as she gazed at the fire. "I can still taste it even after I took the antidote. With that clay and dirt soaking it up, I doubt it'll ever be safe to drink from that water again."

"Can you treat the water to make it safe?" Clint asked Whiteoak.

"I suppose if I dump some of the antidote in there, it should counteract it. I'll deliver the antidote to the other towns along that creek myself just to be certain."

"Folks forget," Jenny said. "Someone will come back and camp on that ground sometime. Do you even know if that stuff will . . . I don't know . . . fade away?"

Whiteoak shrugged. "It would be best to keep people

away from there for a good, long while. Just to be on the
safe side."

Nodding, Clint said, "I think I have an idea."

Clint didn't leave Piedmont for a few weeks. He stayed behind to make certain all of Colfield's men were gone, and
didn't run into a single one of them. Sheriff Morton might
have been on Teasley's payroll, but he was able to deal with
any of the hired guns Teasley's boys had missed.

The rest of his time was spent with Jenny and Whiteoak
making rides into the desert to harvest a very specific sort
of crop. Besides being a very dangerous crop, it was also
difficult to transport since it didn't particularly enjoy being
plucked from the rocks and tossed into a sack.

Clint rode to the creek with the last of those sacks,
opened it, and turned it upside down. Four rattlesnakes
dropped to the clay and hissed loudly at Clint before slithering off toward the bushes. Like all the other snakes
they'd dropped off, these instinctively avoided the charred
remains of the spot where Colfield had made his last stand.

The whole area no longer felt dead. On the contrary, it
felt alive and slithering as the snakes had already started
building their homes and burrowing into the dirt outside
the clay-packed shore. Clint steered Eclipse well away
from the creek and snapped the reins, leaving behind a
whole mess of rattlers as well as plenty of signs around the
perimeter of that area.

The signs read:

SNAKEBITE CREEK
KEEP AWAY

It wasn't perfect, but it would have to do. For Clint, that
was plenty.

J. R. ROBERTS

THE GUNSMITH

LONGARM

**Explore the exciting Old West with one
of the men who made it wild!**

GIANT-SIZED ADVENTURE FROM
AVENGING ANGEL LONGARM.

Longarm and the
Outlaw Empress
0-515-14235-2

When Deputy U.S. Marshal Custis Long stops a
stagecoach robbery, he tracks the bandits to a town
called Zamora. A haven for the lawless, it's ruled by
one of the most powerful, brilliant, and beautiful women in
the West...a woman whom Longarm will have to face, up
close and personal.